DISTURBING THE PEACE

CAROLINE WOODWARD

POLESTAR
BOOK PUBLISHERS

Published by
Polestar Press Ltd., R.R. 1, Winlaw, B.C., V0G 2J0, 604-226-7670
Distributed by
Raincoast Book Distribution Ltd., 112 East 3rd Avenue,
Vancouver, B.C., V5T 1C8, 604-873-6581
Published with the assistance of the Canada Council

Canadian Cataloguing in Publication Data
Woodward, C. Hendrika, 1952—
Disturbing the peace
ISBN 0-919591-53-1
I. Title.
PS8595.059D5 1990   C813'.54   C90-091151-4
PR9199.3.W65D5 1990

Acknowledgements
The author wishes to thank the Canada Council Explorations
Program and the Ontario Arts Council, Writers Reserve Fund
Program, for their support.
Many thanks are also due to the following individuals and agen-
cies who have provided encouragement and expertise along the
way: Paulette Jiles, Colin Browne, Pauline Butling, Fred Wah,
Kathy Scardellato, John Newlove, Rita Moir, Dave Lewis,
Maureen Wilson, Anne Snider, Clark Blaise, Joan Webb, Don
Barz, Perth friends, the Hudson Bay Archives in Winnipeg,
G.P.V. and Helen B. Akrigg's *British Columbia Place Names*,
Mum, Mi, Davy, Shani, and especially Seamus and Jeff George.

Roy Forbes has kindly allowed the use of words from his song
"Farmer Needs The Rain"©Roy Forbes, Casino Music, PRO.

Some of these stories have appeared in the following magazines
and anthologies. The author is very grateful for the support
shown her work by *The Malahat Review, PRISM international,
Images, This Magazine, Canadian Fiction Magazine, Imagining
Women, Between You Me And The Stars,* and
Frictions: Stories By Women.

Produced by Polestar in Winlaw, B.C.
Printed and bound in Canada

Disturbing the Peace is the fourth title in the Polestar First Fiction
series, a series that showcases new Canadian writing by publishing the writer's first novel or collection of short stories.

*This book is dedicated to the memory of my wonderful Dad,
David Morgan Woodward (1914-1984),
and to the magnificent river that once was the Peace.*

Contents

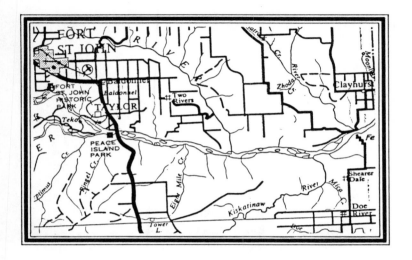

Peace River Block

I can't go home again. I mean it.
The winters are too long & too cold up north.
Even chinooks won't tempt me.
It suits me to look at my maps,
to spread them all around me.

Some of the places disappear from one map
to the next. Poof!
Gone without a trace or a ripple
or a peep. Blown off the map.

For these places, the ghosts
of one-room schools
abandoned gas pumps
flooded Indian pack trails—
I dedicate this record of the Peace River Block.
The names can be chanted or read silently
or sung to the tune you hear when you stretch out
on the ground with one ear pressed firmly to the Earth.

Listen. Alces, Arras, Aitken Creek, Altona.
Attachie for the Chief who signed Treaty 8.
Baldonnel for Ballydonnel in one Old Country
& Bear Flat for the bears, with beautiful black soil
B.C. Hydro wants four fathoms down & Blueberry River
for the berries there. Bessborough. A stately name
for two gravel roads intersecting & Buick Creek,
a mysterious name of unknown origins, though I fancy
a homesteader's vintage Buick high-centred, with
water rising past the doors, well over the running boards.
Boundary Lake on the border & the lean brown Beatton
River for Frank Wark Beatton, Orkneyman &
Hudson Bay factor.

Onward. Cecil Lake. My first home, the place
of my parents' homestead on the banks of the Beatton.
Surveyed in 1912, a glorified slough really,
until Major Cecil Mortimer called it his own.
Migrating birds pay their respects en route & once,
buffalo bones were found on the bottom during a drought.
Charlie Lake. Now here's another. Some know
Charlie Yahey, maybe the last Prophet of the Beaver.
Well, this lake is named for his father, Charlie Chokaka
a.k.a. Big Charlie.

PEACE RIVER BLOCK

Clayhurst where the cable ferry across the Peace River
used to be, Clayhurst for William Clay.
Dog River, Doig River, Two Rivers, Sweet Water.
Erin Lea, the school long-gone, the name bestowed
by Old Mr. Cuthbert, the Irish patriarch
who could sometimes be persuaded to rise
from the bench in the Cecil Lake Hall to recite
poetry from where he stood. Epic poetry!
The voices in the Hall calling out, urging him on,
requesting their favourites by Tennyson & Yeats.
Flatrock, Golata Creek for Frank Golata,
Goodlow for Jim Good and Mrs. Low.
Moose Creek & Snoose Creek & Spence's Creek
with a rough log bridge full of holes to catch
a clumsy horse foot like our Brownie's.
A bridge to tense up the team & the driver,
plunging down the short steep bank, bang, bang, bang
on the bridge & up the other bank,
horses lunging in their harness, us cheering!

Some of these names are so small, so local, the creeks
so seasonal they are never more than a thin blue line
on maps of the imperfect present
or the recent past.
Now, instead of riding horses to school, the kids ride
huge buses for mile after hour after mile
to huge rural schools like Clearview where there are
gymnasiums instead of rabbit traplines
to tend to at noon hour.

But now to the drowned places. Je me souviens.
Lest we forget.
Branham, Beattie, Cust & Gold Bar.

CAROLINE WOODWARD

Morgan Flats, Indian Head Flats & most of Elizabeth Creek.
Elizabeth. Lizzie. Lillibet.
Whoever & wherever are you now?
These are just the English underwater.

Ne Parle Pas Point preserves the memory of rapids
so quiet, so lethal on the Peace that
voyageurs made myths of them, those 18th Century
Quebecois so skillful with canoes. Maybe they made
bad jokes, a rough translation of which I'll kindly provide:
"Don't look now but we're smack in the middle
of those no-noise rapids, Alphonse!" & Alphonse
would berate Phillipe: "Don't speak up now,
Monsieur Avengle! (Blind-As-A-Bat!)
You missed the little arrow to the portage again,
O Chalice! darn you, O Tabernacle, darn you,
O Saint's Bones, etc." & then they'd both
paddle like hell to prevent their imminent
deaths from occuring. Who knows how many languages
are drowned down there where the Bennett
& Peace Canyon Dams hover?

I cannot speak for the Beaver, the Cree, the Sikanni.
I do not know their places where saskatoons were best
where deer came to the salt licks
where a person could sit & get magic
or where the Finlay & Parsnip met, fringed by giant
cow parsnip, Indian rhubarb, seven feet high but that
doesn't matter anymore
for Finlay Forks is underwater.
I can say I swam there once, in Lake Williston,
June, 1969. I floated face-down
over a forest of stumps in water so green & clear.

PEACE RIVER BLOCK

Onward. I want to rise above ground
to Farrel Creek, Farmington, Fellers Heights
& Fort St. John, a manic depressive kind of town
with highs & lows like everybody's business.
Land of the New Totems
which are oil & gas derricks
standing tall on this northern prairie.
Once the stomping grounds of Ma Murray, it's got
two hockey rinks, a pretty good Stampede in July,
the Mukluk Rendezvous & a giant mosquito mascot.

I want to cite every one-pump podunk place
in the boonies of the Peace River Block, the last
Canadian frontier except, of course,
the human mind.
Each place name a metaphor, a simile, or a fact
of physical geography. Sometimes, a straightforward
possessive as in Tom's Lake or Hudson's Hope.
There is nostalgia aplenty for places left behind
like Rolla, Missouri, which is named for Raleigh,
North Carolina by a Missourian who couldn't spell
but what the hell, eh?

My favourites are the anecdotal, the episodic names,
the names that call out loud & clear:
"Something happened here, here ye, hear ye!"
Like the one for a small lake where evangelists set up
a camp & congregated by the dozens for the total immersion
method of baptism which provoked the local wags
to remark that a great deal of sin must have been washed
off there, & so they called it Sin Lake.
Getting back to dry land, I call upon the collective

memories of Groundbirch, East Pine, Pineview, North Pine
with its wonderful fair & Rose Prairie so famous
for its dancers making the little hop in the two-step,
for the four-handed schottische & pump-handled waltzers.
Also Montney, Muirdale, Milligan Creek & Prespatou.
Sing out Gundy & Tupper & Moberly too! Toast the
Industrial Giants! Chetwynd, formerly Little Prairie,
Taylor Flats for Herbie Taylor, proudly proclaiming itself
the Pittsburgh of the North.

There are memorials to royalty, surveyors & others
less than savoury though someone had the good sense
to convert Mount Stalin to Mount Peck for us to remember
guide & outfitter Don Peck. R.I.P.
Hail, also, to Sikanni Chief River in memory
of Makenunatane, the greatest Prophet of the Dunne-za,
Real People, known to whites as the Sikanni Chief
of the Beaver Indians.

There is no statue of George Herbert Dawson,
Skookum Tum Tum. Sikanni for Brave & Cheerful One,
a minute, meticulous hunchback circa 1879
who surveyed most of this country in the South Peace
& for whom Dawson Creek is named.
City of elevators, one of which is an art gallery,
Dawson Crick, home of the Mile Zero Post &
CJDC Radio & T.V. where we watched my cousin
do the Twist in 1965 while the Nighthawks were playing
on the Teen Town Show & we were all so excited.

Romantics & farmers have much in common. Give a listen.
Sunrise Valley, Sundance, Sunset Prairie & Progress.
Kilkerran, Shearer Dale, Halfway River & Upper Cutbank.

PEACE RIVER BLOCK

Peace River, itself, Mother Water, Unchagah,
where the Beaver & Cree ended their warring in 1790.
Kiskatinaw River, Cree for cutbank, Sukunka Falls
& River, a best-kept secret of the north,
Portage Mountain, Pink Mountain, Mount Gething for
King Gething, the coal-mining man. Tumbler Ridge,
instantville, where stocks & fortunes soar, stagger
& tumble at the taxpayer's expense.

Now, Fort Ware looks out on a lake instead of a valley
& the Graham River, settled by new religious colonies,
flows in memory of Lt. J.R. Graham, surveyor, killed
in France, World War I. All these names, these places,
these lives & deaths, live in spidery script on old maps
or surface boldly in the '80's.

Finally, Pouce Coupe.
Eastern Canadian announcers make jokes
about Pouce Coupe & mispronounce it while they're at it.
We say *poos koopee* not *puce kupay* or some such rubbish.
But let that go. There was a fine Sikanni trapper
who blew off one thumb in a gun accident & the voyageurs
nicknamed him Pouce Coupe. His real name is forgotten.
But he is mentioned by Simon Fraser in his journals (1806)
& what's more, there is a Cut Thumb Creek
that flows into the Parsnip & a whole town named for him.
We remembered. We named this place.

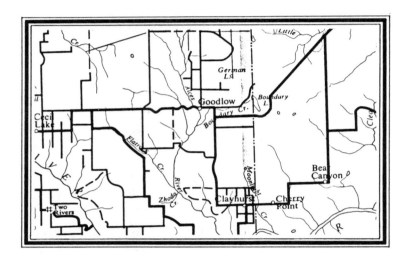

Imagining Autobiography

(1954 & 1974)

The wheat is taller than me, and I am running to Isabel's place. My toes are sinking into dust, stubbing on stalks. I have bloomers on and some light little shirt and the sun is hot. The clacking of grasshoppers is everywhere and I stir them up as I run. They fly up and bash into my legs and face. This is my first moving footage, my first movie starring me.

It must have been August for the wheat to have such heavy heads. I duck my head down and keep running, trying to pull the stalks aside, to keep their small and spiky beards from getting my face. Behind me some grown-ups are talking on the road about rain. Or bushels to the acre. These voices mix into the grasshoppers, droning and clacking.

The road they are standing on splits at the first gate and goes through bush on the left to Murphy's place and through four gates on the right until it gets to the road which goes up to the highway. I don't think I knew about the roads or the gates then, on the day I started running to Isabel's. I am two and a half. No one else remembers any of it.

Straight across this field of wheat, through the barbwire fence, more field (oats?), some bush, then barnyard, is Isabel's place. We can see the light of her kitchen from our livingroom window. She sits on her high kitchen chair by her window and smokes and always has raisin cookies. Once I had canned bear meat she made. Someone mentions her name, one of the visitor grown-ups, and I go running to see her. Isabel lets me sit on her lap and I sing songs for her and she claps for me.

□   □   □

Once I paid for a glider ride, towed up to 2500 feet by a small plane and then let go. There was a handsome pilot and me behind him like the Red Baron and Snoopy. The pilot's name was Red, in fact, and he used to have a teen radio show on CKNL Wide Sky Radio called Rockin' Red Ryder (590 on your dial). Then he got too old for that and started flying anything for anybody. Two-bit bush plane outfits forever going down in godforsaken places but that came later.

On this day we are floating and bouncing up hundreds of feet on thermal updrafts from the hot brown summer-

CAROLINE WOODWARD

fallow below. We slip along completely without sound except for me going "Wow Wow" and Red saying "We gotta good run here," and "Wanna go there?" pointing to the river. For an ex-deejay he didn't talk much.

We hover over the Beatton River, see the bridge, see where the river runs into the Peace, brown on brown, the Peace swallowing the lean brown ribbon of the Beatton without so much as a burp. We do a complete 360 degree flip and I screech the "f" word, which I hardly ever said, and which I did then to impress Red with my sophistication. He just laughs a bit and says not to worry when I apologized (to cover all my bases in case he preferred more innocent types) because just about everyone swears at 360s. We do two more at my request and I keep my eyes open and watch our fixed wing shadow on the ground below. The sun is just right for shadows.

□ □ □

I hear someone hollering my name and yoohooing. I stop running and look up and all I can see is high blue sky. Then the world swirls and someone (my Dad) picks me up, laughing, saying, "She would have made it all the way to Isabel's!" (But I did, I did!) I didn't know the word for flying, I just pointed and said, "Up! Up!"

This is where my memory begins.

□ □ □

The last time we climbed up, I stretched my arms out wide, pressed my hands up against the glass bubble, counted to eight for as long as I saw sky only, and there it was, the airstrip below and me made wide and open above.

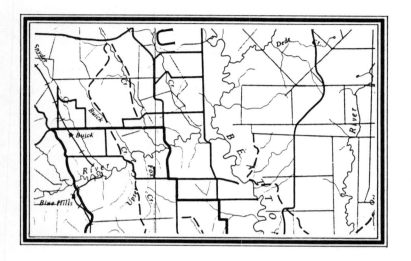

Farm Stuff

There was underwear, one family's worth, minus the father's, on four clotheslines packed with towels and kids' overalls and her housedresses with sweat stains ringed around the armpits. The torn stuff, whites gone yellow or grey, and unmentionables were put behind on the fourth line, hidden from visitors or people on Sunday drives or simply lost, turning their cars at the dead end of a gravel road.

Our house was moved here by trucks from some other place way back off the road. It still perched on eight stacks of wood blocks. Our house looked like a pale orange and turquoise hen about to set on eggs, caught halfways in the final hunker down. This fall we had to get money to hire somebody with a couple of house jacks to lower it down on cement blocks which we also had to get from town, I guess. The right thing would be to have a cement foundation poured and to set the house down neat-as-can-be on top of that. We'd be lucky to get hold of the blocks and get the house banked up with dirt and rocks before freeze-up. Vicky said our house was moved to the end of this road for the sake of improvements. She'd heard people say that if everyone lived on a road it wouldn't cost as much.

For what? I asked. What is going to improve, us being on the road? The bus, for starters, she says. It'll have to turn around here and we can watch in the mornings from the window by the couch for the lights to get to Mikelson's hill and then we'll get on our boots and coats and hop on it right outside our door. That's as far as it went. If Vicky knew more about improvements, she wasn't saying. So we waited.

And once, a city woman, stylish, fiftyish, gets out to use our facilities. A washroom. She is red-faced, glistening. Toilet! she almost snaps.

We stand in a stupid hickish clump until Vicky says some polite thing about first asking Momma? Who is hiding behind the porch door again.

Well, says the lady, she'll be quick, no question, it's urgent, unless our mother is in the bath just now?

All four of us tense up. We don't have facilities or wash-rooms or anything like that inside. Ours is a two-holer back behind the clothesline. It really stinks in the summer,

FARM STUFF

no matter how much wood ash gets dumped down the holes.

She doesn't say anything more, just stands still and watches us. There is one long beat with nothing but the purr of the big black Lincoln and grasshoppers clacking.

We'll have to show you, ma'am, says Vicky and leads the way with the lady, half-trotting in her high heel strappy shoes, then the three of us coming along behind them. We stop at the end of the clothesline and watch her make it the rest of the way on her own, Vicky pointing at the tarpaper shack. She puts her head down and runs, making funny little hops to clear the anthill and the wild rose branches straggling onto the trail. Vicky turns and shoos us all back out of sight.

We go back to the house in time to see Momma skirting the potato patch, heading for the calf barn again. Just as well, really.

The door of the shitter slams, bam, bam. Deedee and Dwight break into a little confused run going nowhere. Vicky snags them by the straps and hauls them back to where we were all standing when we started this. Which is in front of the house looking at the big black car coming down the road to see if it was lost or if it was just some people driving around looking at places.

I say out loud that I don't want to talk to the lady after she comes out of that stinkhole. You never have to do the talking anyway, so shut right up says Vicky in her most mean voice. The twins go to put their hands on the car because of the dust all over it, and Vicky and I break off from each other and go haul them away from it.

They are going through a phase about seeing their two sets of handprints side by side in all sorts of substances.

They are mad four-year-old scientists with experiments in mud, cowshit, tomato guts and saskatoon juice.

The city woman runs by, her face back to a normal colour, saying thanks, saved my day! She waves, gets into the Lincoln (there is a blast of violin-type music), shuts the door, thuck, peels out, spraying gravel, drives up the road leaving a thick cloud of dust we could follow for two and a half miles. That's how we knew people were coming so far in advance.

So. Vicky and I look at each other and do a mind-read and break into a run at exactly the same second.

She left a dollar bill in the box nailed to the wall where the asswipe was kept. Vicky got it. Longer arms. But I spotted the writing.

"KNOWLEDGE IS POWER"
(Sir Francis Bacon)

Right there beside the box in ballpoint blue pen.

We jump out to get away from the stink, even though we couldn't help noticing the ashcan was emptied right out. She must have known to do that herself. There was a faint haze of ash dust still hanging in the air. We ran to hide between two rows of sheets hanging on the lines.

We could hear Momma yodelling down by the calves. So she was fine. We had a while to talk but not long. The twins could wander off to the scoop-out and drown in two minutes.

The dollar we would keep for her Christmas present. First choice was a Wilf Carter record. (He took all her 33's just because we couldn't even run a player out here, he said, but it was the meanest thing he could do when he

FARM STUFF

left and he knew it.) Second choice was a new set of Sunday (white) to Saturday (red) panties to replace the set that was all worn out and full of holes, pinned behind the sheets so visitors couldn't see them from the road.

Vicky put the dollar in her hanky until we scouted a better place to hide it. (The chicken house, under a tobacco can overturned in the farthest corner under the roosts.)

I used to go back and sit and look at her writing. I could not figure it. Our place did not have the power yet. Nobody on this road did. The poles only went as far as the other side of the river to the bridge.

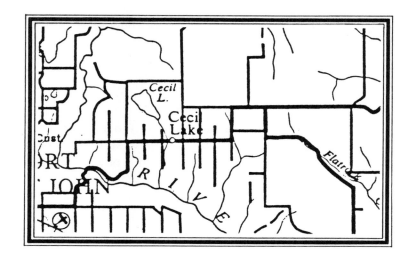

Caboose

The book hit the biggest pile of crap and did one slow end-over-end before coming to rest af an angle against the smaller pile. I held the second one for several more seconds. This cover was my favourite, all marbled shades of palest turquoise, old roses and cream. My aim was better. It bounced off the divider planks between the grown-up hole and the kid's hole and ricocheted completely out of sight. So much for *Through The Looking Glass*.

Alice In Wonderland, all mint greens and silvery orange swirls, nestled right on top of the torn newspapers and crap directly below. I needed a long stick to poke it completely out of sight. No time for that. I grabbed some pages out of *The Western Producer*, crumpled them up and let them waft down for eight feet. Blue-backed flies rose up slowly and settled back sticky-footed. Some leggy mosquitos whined and circled uselessly.

Not good enough. The book still peeked out plain as day. Like some kind of precious egg in a fouled nest. And I heard them running down the trail to the outhouse. So I grabbed the five gallon ash pail and tipped it over the hole, covering the whole pile with chunks of black wood carbon and grey ash. I yanked at my pants and plunked myself down to trap the thick billows rising up fast.

"Is that you in there?"

My sister.

"You can wait!"

"Where's your kissy book?"

My brother.

"I don't have a kissy book! Get out of here, you creeps!"

"Marnie's got a kissy book!"

"Marnie's got a lovey book!"

I peed and cried and wished they'd die.

"Hurry up in there you kids!"

Our Dad. Good.

I zipped up and snuck out while Dad stood, with his back still turned, about fifteen feet away. They'd all scrammed, and I could hear them shrieking and ki-yi-ing over by the gas barrels.

For the next two days, I ran there, sometimes ten times a day, to inspect. I stood over the holes and squinted from all angles, but they were gone completely, no hard edges, no lovely marbled colours, all gone.

"Is your tummy upset, Marnie?"

My mother. She's dying to know if I've gotten the Period and haven't gotten around to telling her yet. Nadine should get it first, by rights, she's nineteen months older than me and all that. Besides, I'm not even twelve, so it's just plain ridiculous to keep bugging me about the dumb thing.

Back to my *Alice* books. I sweated it out for a week but they'd forgotten about them by the looks of it. So no one else would come across Tanya and Doctor Bill saying "I Love You" and "I Love You, Too." "Always" and "Everlasting," etc. I drew Tanya in long evening gowns and Doctor Bill with a stethoscope. They were In True Love and they were Mine Forever, or just for a while the way this worked out. I could of written a full-length book, I was just getting started. I needed blank paper, and that's how this *Alice* book business got me in trouble.

When it was winter, before we got the car, we went up to the Co-op in the caboose Dad built before the war. It took a team of horses to pull it, and all five of us could sit in it on the benches along two sides. It looked like a little grey house with a couple of holes drilled through for the harness lines. The small tin heater would warm us up in no-time-flat, all crammed together with blankets over our knees and our feet up on hot bricks in gunny sacks.

It was eight miles to the store, a four-hour round trip, not counting an hour to shop, get the mail and visit at the Co-op. On the way back home, we would start to fall asleep and end up amongst the bags of groceries, blankets over us, the caboose just rocking from side to side down the road home, the horse harness jangling, the wood sap popping in the heater, and the sleigh runners squeaking on the dry snow. It would be dark by then, mid to late afternoon, and inside the caboose with no windows, you could just see the end of Dad's cigarette and the red of the stovepipe when the heater was going full blast.

The caboose was off its sleigh runners and sitting on the far side of the main garden beside the rhubarb during the summers, so it was a perfect play house. I found the grown-up comic book on the bench one summer before I could read. I must of been five. I sat beside the rusty heater and made up stories to go with each page of pictures.

"Tanya, will you come with me and be my bride?"

"Wherever are you going, Doctor Bill?"

"To Africa. I need a nurse."

"Sure, Doctor Bill. We can ride elephants."

"Fine. Let me call the army."

Then play-acting from one side of the caboose to the other, being Doctor Bill on one side and Tanya on the other. All the comic book pictures were of soldiers in jungles or inside tanks and except for Tanya, there were no other girls in the book. Tanya was with Doctor Bill at the beginning and at the end. The soldiers were in the middle. I had an old curtain for Tanya's dress and one of Dad's ripped shirts for my Doctor Bill part. I brought in sealers of Indian paintbrush and stolen sweetpeas for play days.

Once, I sat there holding Tanya and Doctor Bill close to me, and I got all warm and heavy down there. I could read some of the comic book by then and they really did say "I Love You" and Doctor Bill carried Tanya in his arms to cross a river. THE END. Tanya lying back, eyes closed, catalogue-lady breasts in the air. Doctor Bill with his big arms, hairy chest, and huge, square jaw with a dimple in

CAROLINE WOODWARD

the middle. The heaviness started below my tummy and spread down my legs. I leaned back feeling dizzy and hot, in waves coming up to my neck. I had to jump up to stop it. I stepped outside the caboose and it was all the same, a hot August day, a wind ruffling the poplar leaves, the good smell of alfalfa cut and drying. The screen door banged at the house.

I went back in and hid the comic book in the stove pipe and got rust all over my hands. The very next day, Dad tore down the caboose because he needed the boards to build something else. I don't know what ever happened to the heater. That all happened four years ago. I wanted us to have another caboose, but the open sleigh could hold more stuff like wood and hay. Besides, we were going to get a car and go to the Co-op in style. What a joke. The Chev wouldn't start half the time when it was colder than ten below. They'd bring the battery inside and try and warm it up beside the stove. They hitched the team to it and everyone would push and see if the motor would turn over once we got the thing moving. We'd have to wait out the cold spells, getting really low on groceries until a trip to the store was absolutely necessary. We froze our faces and ran behind the open sleigh to stop our feet from freezing up solid. Then us kids who couldn't keep up to the sleigh would howl, pointing to our frost patches, *white ears*, even. Thawing out was the worst. I'm saying we should of kept the caboose and we'd be happy and warm.

What I did was to write and draw on all the blank pages at the front and back of the *Alice* books my godmother had given me for my birthday. I brought Tanya and Doctor Bill back into my life. I wanted them to be together in the jungles of Africa, saving lives. I started out with words and

I should of stopped there. But I drew their pictures too and more words in bubbles from their mouths, with thought bubbles coming from their eyes.

"Tanya, I need a nurse." *(Be my bride!)*

"Let's go to Africa tomorrow." *(Marry me!)*

"Tanya, you are beautiful." *(I love you forever!)*

Well, Nadine borrowed the books without asking and found out about my love story. She had forgotten how earlier that summer we had played in the empty pig-house, putting wild flowers all over it. And how we danced with crooked sticks we called Jimmy and Bobbie. Our grooms. Our weddings with wild bluebells and goldenrod bouquets. Me carrying her over the front step of the pig-house. Her carrying me, head back, throat exposed, eyes closed, almost. She had a bad habit of dropping me without warning when her arms were tired.

But now Nadine is thirteen, and she and her buddies in Grade Seven talk about boys non-stop. She wouldn't even look at me with her friends around at recess and noon-hour. All they ever did was dangle on the big swings, giggling about boys, and going to live in the dorm for high school in town and having boyfriends and going to dorm dances. I still had forts of moss, hay, sticks and snow. I had my own gang, and we took any boys prisoner if they entered our territory in the bush behind the school. We made them confess to spying and say they were sorry twenty-five times. Then we let them go.

Nadine remembered my love story when I refused to dry dishes for the third day in a row. I'd paid her back, and it was my turn to wash. But she had stored it up.

"Hey, Mom? Marnie drew kissing pictures all over her birthday books!"

"What? What? Did you go and use bad words?" asked Mother, her eyes gone piggy. "Hey? Hey? You watch out." I don't remember what I said. I screamed at them both for making everything dirty and bad. I got slapped and sent outside.

I need a book with a lock on it, like they have in town stores for my real life and my real stories. It is easiest to stick with Once-Upon-A-Time stuff for school and to wait a while before doing my own stories. This way, I could make a princess, a prince, a fairy godmother, a wicked witch. Stir them up and serve them happy-ever-after. THE END. Draw two gold crowns and a magic wand. Push the old witch into a big hole, where she belonged. THE END. A castle on a hilltop with the sun overhead, all spiky crayon rays and happy days ahead. THE END. etc.

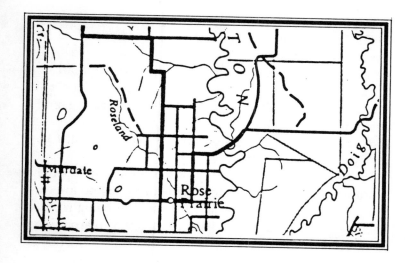

Deliberate

I still get nervous about delivering messages of any great importance. A funny thing happens to my ears. They fill up with the sound of the sea, a real roaring surf, just when I'm trying to keep the facts straight. If someone's eyes get shifty when they're telling me something, or if their hands start wringing and their face changes colour, I'll be busy staring at those things and their words will all run together uselessly. These ears fill up with the tides and the echoes of other tides, and it's just no use telling me anything anymore. I can't help it.

The first time I remember it taking over was when I was in Grade One and having to stand up in front of all four grades in the room. Mr. Abley stood at the front of the room after asking the class to excuse the interruption.

I stood there like I was asked to, what else does a six-year-old do? Mr. Abley the Principal started talking, and it began to sink into me that I was in some kind of trouble. Kids were looking at me sideways, I could tell, but I kept my eyes straight ahead.

"Very! Silly! Little Girl! Who knocked on our door this morning before school started. Who knocked and knocked for at least ten minutes! And why was she being so silly? Because she and her little friend wanted to run around the track. Imagine that! Whoosh, blah, whoosh, blah, whoosh, whoosh...and now you apologize to Mrs. Abley and myself! Emma!"

I am standing beside the wooden desk and staring at the blackboard letters. Big A, little a, Big B, little b. Apple. Ball.

"Can you make a proper apology, Emma? For all that noise this morning?"

"Yes. I can." The roaring is almost over. Whoosh, whoosh. I am almost back to myself, standing, waiting for the right words to come.

"May I say something?"

"That's what we're waiting for. I certainly hope you're not being rude as well as thoughtless, Emma. Just a simple little apology is what we need from you. 'I am sorry for waking you up so early this morning, Mr. and Mrs. Abley.' Now!" Mr. Abley starts out so quiet you can hardly hear him and ends up snarling like Hitler on the radio.

"I am sorry for waking you up this morning to ask permission to run on the track like we were supposed to,

DELIBERATE

Mr. and Mrs. Abley."

His Adam's apple jerks around. He has thin lips without any colour to them and they are twitching up over his teeth now. He looks like a weasel when his teeth show like that. He looks over at Mrs. Abley who has her head down and is patting at her brown wool suit with one hand and rubbing her elbow on the corner of her desk, like she's got an itch. She bobs her head like a bird at him and then she says, in a very small voice, for me to sit down. I do.

He walks back to the big room where he teaches the Grade Fives to Eights without saying anything more. I sneak a look at Dottie but she ducks her head away, gutless little hound. She is always too scared to ask for anything except the bathroom, and so I said I'd ask. It was a rule to ask first because white lime had been put down to make lanes for the runners.

Do Not Run On The Track Unless You Have Permission From Your Teacher. So. I knocked on their teacherage door. I could hear them moving around. I waited. I knocked again. Nothing. Then some mumbling. Dottie wanted to leave. But I heard them in there and kept knocking. My mum and dad would never pretend not to be home if someone was knocking on our door. I kept knocking.

When the door finally opened, Mr. Abley was wearing some kind of plaid housecoat and looked red and angry. He told us to go away unless it was something really important. "May we please run on the track?" I asked. "No, you may not!" he snapped back. Then slammed the door.

I am Emma Jean Martin, oldest daughter of Norah and Matthew Martin, and I was taught to speak up, to not act shy or foolish if I have something to say. So I speak up to ask permission and look what happens! And why do I have to stand up all by myself to take all the blame? I told my dad I'd been asked to say "sorry" to them, but I was supposed to do what I had to turn around and say "sorry" for, and what did he make of that? Dad said there must be more to it than that and thought for a bit more, but that's where he left it. I was glad the Ableys left after that year for a school in the Okanagan, where the weather was so nice.

Our dad taught us all to box barehanded, but kids here in Grade Eight don't fight fair. They kick each other in the crotch, wearing heavy boots. Boys pull at each other's you-know-whats. Girls sharpen their nails and bite like wolverines, anywhere they can get a grip. Families have to look out for each other, and friends had better be loyal or else they're not friends for long.

My ears fill up for fights, but that is a blessing. I shut out the screams of the big circle of kids surrounding us and concentrate on getting the boy more scared of me than I am of him. Once I fought a boy for giving my sister Janey a bloody nose, because she was one year younger than him and a foot smaller. It was an accident, but he wasn't sorry about it, so I went after him. My worst fight was with Steve Mosely, who punched my horse in the nose after offering it some grass to eat. Steve's ugly and known for his mean streak, but I didn't care. I punched and punched him until he curled up on the ground. He tortures animals every chance he gets, but that was the last time he went near mine. My ears roared and my eyes got sharp, and I didn't stop until it was clear he was scared crapless of me.

DELIBERATE

But the time I broke through the roaring and knew the true thing was when I heard someone else's roaring for the first time and joined in. Yesterday, it was. February 13, 1958. We were all on the school bus, coming home on the East Run, with about twenty of us on board. The bus smells like orange peels and gum and sweaty kids with not so clean hair. There's someone eating sandwiches with sardines right behind me. We aren't supposed to eat on the bus but nobody tells, and Mr. Carew is too kind to yell about kids being hungry on his bus. It takes an hour to get home for our family.

Janey, Stefan and I get out with the Samson kids at the turnaround on the end of our road. Mr. Carew kept looking at me in the mirror and when we get out, he asks me to wait.

"You tell your Dad we need him at the cemetery tomorrow, okay, Emma? About one o'clock with his pickaxe?"

I stare up at him and start to ask, but before I get past "Who...", he tips his head back a little and leans toward me.

"It's someone on the bus," he whispers. "Tomorrow at one, alright? There's a good girl."

I watch the bus make the turnaround and send up a double spray of flying snow behind the chained-up wheels. I turn around and look at four light blue eyes above two identical dark green scarves.

"What did Mr. Carew want?" asks Janey.

"Nothing for your ears, Nosey Parker," I say, knowing she will frost her lungs to get ahead at the last gate so she can tell Dad first. We aren't supposed to run when it's cold. We're supposed to walk with scarves over our noses and mouths.

I start to walk on the road home without saying another word to them. The road is drifted solid in lots of places, hard-packed enough to walk on, so it's easy going. I can hear Janey and Stefan behind me, yelling at me to slow down, but I don't. I need to think by myself.

Someone on the bus. I think back, seat by seat, seeing the faces of the Mennonite kids, the McManus sisters, the mill kids from the North Road, then the boys from the Tolmey ranch, two by two. The cousins from the Big Hill, the Metis boy living at Swanson's farm, the Samsons, everyone was there. I, myself, had done the attendance for the Grades One to Fours this morning as part of the teacher's assistant duties. My neat red checkmarks on the ledger at five past nine, right after the Lord's Prayer and Bible reading, float past my brain. Even though the morning started out at 25 below, the school's propane tank hadn't gelled and the school was warm. There was perfect attendance. I was positive of it.

Mr. Carew didn't mean it was a school kid, he meant it was someone's family.

My lungs start to hurt, and my scarf is wet from my breath and freezing solid. I should slow down after the first gate. It is half buried in drifts and a hard, crusty bank of old snow left by the grader. Why he can't move the blade just a little and not bury the gate is a mystery. I have to gouge out a hole where I think the barbwire loop is circled around the stick and pull the other poles, and the mess of wire stapled to them, out of the packed snow. Or else we could ignore the gate and carefully squeeze through between two wires, everyone helping so our parkas and hats

DELIBERATE

don't get caught in the barbs.

Stefan is crying hard when he and Janey get to the gate. I mop at his face with a dry part of my scarf.

"Stop bawling, Stefan! I'll slow down and walk with you the rest of the way," I say, but he keeps on howling. "Do you need to go number one?" asks Janey. "Just go over there if you do. We'll wait. Just shut up!"

"My feet!" he gets out, finally. "My boots are frozen up!"

Janey and I get to work. We empty his boots of crammed-in snow, pull up both pairs of socks, and buckle his boots up tightly. He's in Grade Three and young for his grade, just hopeless at dressing himself.

We start out on the last stretch between the spruce, where hardly any snow gets through to the ground and it always feels warmer than the open grain fields we've just crossed. Then we put our heads down for the really windy part, across the alfalfa field and up the big hill to our house. By now, just past four o'clock, it is almost dark. The snow has blue shadows on it, like skim milk. Somewhere back in the muskeg, a tree pops like a rifle shot from the cold. Our boots squeak on the snow, and all of our feet are cold, so there's no use complaining to anyone else. Sam comes running down the hill, barking and jumping all over us, as we climb the very last, very hardest stretch. The wind is up and slices through our homeknit scarves like icy needles. Stefan sobs about every third step he takes. Janey and I will get heck for it. Poor baby Stefan. Four foot zip with a yap down to his ankles.

It could be a car accident. Nobody's parents are old enough to up and die in a day. Or it could be a house fire, like Mr. Kowalchuk, burned on his own couch, never even woke up, people said. As if they could tell. The river road was bound to be icy with the chinook melting so much last week and then the fresh snow covering up all the ice this week. *Tomorrow. One o'clock. Pick-axe.* We finally get to our house, stumble through the porch, and make it into the kitchen. Our house is beautiful and warm with the smells of fresh bread and roasting meat and neatsfoot oil. There is harness spread everywhere because this is Dad's week to mend and clean horse harness, in case he goes up to skid with our team at the sawmill in March. We pull off our parkas and sweaters and double pairs of mitts and all the rest of our gear. Then we sit down at the table.

My tea cup gets forgotten in all the commotion, and I sit there in a daze. Surf's up. Everyone else is diving into tea and buns.

"I don't have my tea yet," I announce and take a big breath. "Dad, Mr. Carew wants you to come to the cemetery tomorrow, around one o'clock, with the pick-axe."

For once our family is quiet. Mum pours my tea and nearly spills some, watching Dad instead of my cup.

"Who's dead, then?" Dad asks. Mum passes me a bun with lots of apple and strawberry jam on it.

"He said it was somebody on the bus so he couldn't tell me, somebody's relative it has to be, not a kid," I say. Suddenly I am very thirsty and very hungry. I've said what I had to, I said it right, no ocean brains.

"We're going to need a lot of tires to burn over this one," Dad says. "Pass the butter please. This'll take two days to dig with the ground frozen down four feet at least, wait and see."

DELIBERATE

Mum makes shushing noises at Dad. Sam starts barking his head off, and we all shut up to listen. A low rumbling noise, ever so faint, fades in and out. Dad gets up and peers through the livingroom window. It's hard to see through the plastic because the frost has turned almost all of it white, except for a clear spot nearer to the heater.

"One headlight and, from the sounds of it, I'd say that's Casey's truck coming," he reports. "Yes, it's him, bringing the news on this, I'll bet you money."

Mum stands up from the table. "Right then, kiddos, chores!" We are shooed outside in a hurry, pulling on our old chore coats.

While Janey and Stefan head to the barn to throw out hay to the cattle, I collect eggs. I take the flashlight and find five eggs in the dark hen boxes, three of them with frozen egg yolks protruding from their split shells. I tuck them into the side pocket of my parka and put a tobacco can of wheat into the halved car tire. The water in the other half of the tire is already frozen, but Mum will bring out warm water in the morning. The chickens are already up on the roosts, sleepy sing-songy noises coming from the mounds of red and white feathers all bunched together for warmth.

I go back to the porch and put the eggs in the cream separator bowl so I won't smash them up getting wood. I have egg yolk stains in most of my coat pockets as it is.

Janey and I haul heater wood from the pile onto the tobaggan and pack them beside the woodbox in the porch. Stefan puts stove wood on his sleigh and crams them into the woodbox. I straighten out the bottom of the next pile of heater blocks and put kindling close to the kitchen door. Then I hear the talking.

"Found him less than a mile up from the Kramer place!"
That was Casey.
"Now why on earth would he break trail down a cutline
instead of walking a bit extra on ploughed road?" Dad.
"Deliberate! If you ask me, that's what it was. Stupid
bugger." That awful Casey again.
"It's not a nice way to talk about someone, is it now?"
Mum. "Besides, what normal father would do that, leaving
those kids?"
"They're alright, looked after anyway, staying with
Dora and Gord for now. They'll go back to the wife on the
Coast, I imagine," says Casey. I can hear him slurping his
tea right through the door! It must be driving Mum up
the wall.
"Well," begins Dad, "If you ask me, he was not a well
man to begin with. Thin, a T.B. type, and today was no day
to be packing groceries and breaking trail."
"That's what I mean! It's one way to go, just lay down
and let the cold take you!" Casey is bleating, his nasal
voice getting higher and all excited. Ugh. I never did like
him with his turkey neck and beady brown eyes. Turkey
vulture.
I tippytoe out of the porch and head back to the woodpile. I would have to look that up. Deliberate. I was quite
sure it meant that a person planned to do something in
advance, like premeditated murder. And halfway to the
woodpile, I know whose dad it is, and I stop dead.
Today, by the school icehouse, the boy had held Stefan
down while another little creep stuffed snow down his
neck. I was on my way to the girl's toilet when I saw
Stefan's dark green scarf on the snow and heard the
choking sounds. I flew at them, kicking and screaming.

DELIBERATE

One ran off, but I trapped Duane and bashed his head against the hard-packed snow. Stefan rolled away and got up. Duane kicked at me, and I grabbed his leg and bit it, hard.

"Like to die? Suffocate like you tried to do to my little brother? A Grade Five picking on a Grade Three?" I kicked him twice in the bum. He stayed down, so I backed away to look after Stefan.

The blizzard came across the field and into the school yard like a white wall. The first noon-hour bell rang, and I turned back to Duane. He was curled up on the snow where I'd left him. His brown paper lunch bag spilled out beside him and a skinny beet-red leg showed above the gumboot that was nearly off his foot. His eyes were closed, and he didn't move even though the snow was coming down so thick now that I couldn't see more than eight feet away.

"Duane! You're doing this on purpose! The bell rang, you hear!" He still didn't move.

"I'm too tired. I'm just going to stay here and sleep." His skinny face was yellowish and his green eyes looked up at me. Strange, peaceful eyes.

I grabbed his lunch bag and then his right arm and pulled him to his feet. He stood there with a funny smile on his face and took some big, deep breaths. From out of nowhere came the ocean in my ears.

flour   corn syrup   Cheese Whiz   powdered milk   tea
1 can Export tobacco   2 Vogue papers   1 box wooden matches
1 gallon coal oil   charge it, please?

Plain as day, that's what I heard Duane's dad say, but I didn't see him say it. It was his voice. I'm not sure how to explain this. I came to my senses and said something about the bell again. Duane didn't say anything except sorry about ten times while we three walked to the school as fast as we could. I think he likes me even though I weigh a lot more than him.

They have to be the ones. They are the only new kids in our school. Just a father and three boys who fought with each other all the time. Came from the Coast. Nobody else's family fought like that, it scared the rest of us when they started up. We didn't form a ring around them at school, we just left them alone to fight it out. Duane was the youngest, so he got the worst of it.

I shovel off our woodpile so we can get at more blocks underneath. Already we're running low on wood. It had to be them. Him. Lying down in the snow with his groceries. I'd shoved a half-eaten pancake with corn syrup on it back into Duane's lunch bag. Burnt and cold. They lived in two old granaries shoved together, on skids, up on a frozen quarter bought from the old Schumann bachelors. Their mother didn't stay more than a week, was the story. I never even saw what she looked like. Once I heard Dad and Mr. Carew talking about what a lousy deal it was to sell that poor land to such a greenhorn.

Today they aren't on the bus. I wait out by the propane tank near the end of noon hour. Sure enough, Dad and Casey drive by in Casey's old jeep truck with a load of tires on the back. I wave and holler at them, but they don't see me.

I get the big dictionary and find the word just as the first bell rings.

deliberate—a. intentional; considered, not impulsive; slow in deciding, cautious; leisurely   b. not hurried (of movement, etc.)

DELIBERATE

"He leisurely lay down in the snow with his bag of groceries." That doesn't make sense. "He cautiously sank to his knees in the snow." No way. I put the dictionary down.

I feel it again, feel his relief. Putting down the heavy bags, having a little rest, then just stopping, floating away, giving Duane a little visit, so close by, and keeping on going. Who's to know?

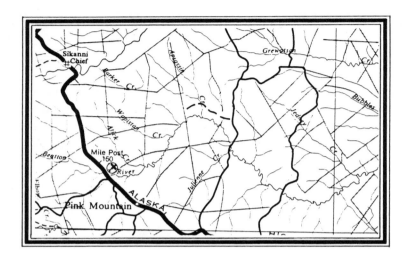

Summer Wages

First off, let's put it into perspective, as Josie used to say.
I, Geraldine, have worked nine waitressing jobs and have
taken the vow never to do it again. Sure, I make these tired
old jokes about support hose and roller skates supplied by
management but I've got other things I can do for less
work and more money. No more shiftwork either.

I do the books for five businesses right out of my own
home. Claim office expenses for one-third of this double-
wide trailer under the self-employed category on income
tax and I sign off with a nice flourish, let me tell you. It's

better that the money comes back to me, hard-working mother of three, than to the lousy government just lusting to squander it on their corrupt friends or some U.S. kick-ass submarine thing.

But here's the kicker. My oldest, Carrie-Lynn, wants to get a job. Fine. Grade ten, smart as a whip, takes after Ab for brains and Josie for looks, like she used to look before she got into the booze. But the job she wants is waitressing up the highway this coming summer. "Just like you and Aunt Josie did."

I'm building up to spilling the beans on her, sitting her down in the next hour when she gets home and telling it like it is. Was, anyway. She's too innocent and the world is meaner and trickier than it was in 1969. I'm going to let loose with the scuzzy side of me and Josie's adventures in Service With A Smileville so she'll clue in and get a decent job. Like being a lifeguard. That's classy and the money is two and a half times minimum wage. She's still got time to get the swim ticket she needs. I'd pay for it, no ifs or buts.

She wouldn't get tips unless she served booze and she's still underage so that's that. The kid's only 15 now, 16 in June, runs like a deer, swims like a guppy, brings home ribbons every sports day and swim meet. Lifeguard badge be a cinch for an athletic kid like her.

Getting the damn pool job is another story though. I got to be realistic on that score. Carrie-Lynn doesn't have a high-up Daddy, or Mommy, to pull strings at City Hall. Ab is the *janitor* at City Hall for crying out loud. Plus he invents things like the automated scarecrow. But until he makes some indecent amount of money, people will just laugh at him. "How's it goin', Ab?" "Built a better mouse-trap yet, Ab?" And Ab will just miss how entirely mean they are and smile and say he's not that interested in mousetraps, his current project is this or that, keeps me busy, keeps me busy, he says, nodding and smiling at the snickering sons of bees. They don't know who they're talking to. Ab's halfways a genius and he's got the kindest heart in the West, not a mean bone in his body. Me, I'm mean, let me tell you.

Me, I should join the Business and Professional Women's Club, get on the power lunch and business card swapmeet circuit but I'm afraid they'd turn me down. I couldn't take that. It kills me because I'm so proud to finally get to be a bookkeeper but that might not be enough for them. A chartered accountant and on up is what to be for them. Carrie-Lynn, Carrie-Lynn, that's where you come in.

I started by default, waitressing, because they hired me to chambermaid. It was new then, it's closed now, a gas station and about ten cabins plus a cafe with a good repu-tation. Exactly halfways between Fort St. John and Fort Nelson with Pink Mountain looming up out of the muskeg some miles away. The Beatton River began a hundred yards from the cafe, just a little brown stream coiling around the willows and stunted spruce trees.

Josie was actually thrilled to be a waitress even when she found out there was no uniform, just a long green apron to tie on over her blouse and jeans. Still, she fixed up her hair and did her nails and worked a full shift an hour after we got there. Petticoat Junction is what the truckers

SUMMER WAGES

called our place on account of the five young women between 16 and 18 that worked there. But by the first of
August, Josie and I were the only employees left. The
Mister had picked a fight with Henry, the gas jockey whose
girlfriend was the head waitress and whose sister was the
second cook. The second cook's best friend was the main
cook, a farm kid from Tom's Lake who had cooked for her
family since she was 11 and that Esther could cook, let
me tell you.

All four of them left in a huff because of Henry being
fired. They headed back to Dawson Creek and big summer
dances with Bim and The Crystal Ship and maybe even
Anthony and The Romans. Lucky bums. We didn't realize
how much fun July had been until we watched them leave
in Henry's souped-up car and the cafe was suddenly dull.
No more Social Centre. Josie and I were on our own with
the Mister and the Wife.

The Mister drank at least once every two weeks and was
out of commission for three or four days at a time. The
Wife was a bible-thumper and an excellent cook but she
holed up in one of the motel units whenever he hit the
bottle so he wouldn't hit her. Josie and I had orders to
leave him be and to bring her meals three times a day. No
problem. We avoided him like the plague, sober or drunk.

We never told our parents. We needed the dollar ten an
hour and all this booze and sex and violence, just like the
TV, only made us feel more grown-up and on our own. We
didn't want to worry the folks. Hear what I'm saying? You
got that little smile on.

So. After the big You're Fired! Like Hell I Am, I Quit!
We All Quit! episode, Josie and I pretty well ran the place.
We'd get up at 5:30 a.m., dash from our unheated shack to

the cafe, get the grill and the coffee on, eat a stack of toast, and go our separate ways. If a tour bus to Fairbanks pulled in, Josie would holler from the back door of the kitchen. I'd set down my toilet scrubber or whatever and run over to ladle out soup and make a bunch more pots of coffee. Josie kept a clean green apron by the door for me so I'd look more or less like a waitress. We'd go flat out getting upward of fifty people fed and watered, answering their dumb questions about where we went to school and how come we didn't have pecan pie and was the soup in the crockpot homemade like the sign hanging over it said?

In July when all five of us had worked, a couple of us could have a break, walk up to the Sikanni Chief airstrip, climb up the old forestry lookout until we lost our nerve around thirty feet up. Henry made it to the top once and so did Josie. It took them forever to get down and I had to run back to cover her shift which pissed me off. It was a whole day off for me and something didn't sit right with me, down on the ground, looking up this ancient creaking tower, and them up there laughing.

Josie and I would hitch the one hundred miles down to Fort St. John every Friday afternoon at four o'clock and on Sunday afternoons we'd hitch back up to work in less than two hours usually. We got rides fast. Two blondes with our thumbs out with no *idea* we were two blondes standing with our thumbs out on the highway! I can't believe it but no kid of mine would stand out there, male or female, not in these times. Only so many angels on duty per innocent kid.

By mid-August we figured out we were putting in close to eighteen-hour days and then it dawned on us we'd just worked seven days a week for two weeks straight. We were missing the really huge parties at the Old Fort and had romances to tend to. Or we liked to think we did. Pink Mountainview Motel or Pink Elephant Lookout as we called it behind the Mister's back was seriously interfering with our futures, and we each had two hundred dollars clear, a small fortune.

Now listen up. Our Dad phoned us right at a busy lunch spell and told us to quit if we'd had enough, give them a week's notice, come home and have a week off before school started. The Wife came in and gave me a dirty look for being on the phone, my only phone call all bloody summer. So I looked at her, said "Uh, huh," when Dad said goodbye and then I said, "Dead?! Where?" Beat. "Mile 109? Mile 136? Omigod!" Beat. "Hitch-hikers? Have they got the murderer yet?" Beat. "Okay. Yes. Okay. Yes, we will. Bye Dad."

The Wife pretended she wasn't eavesdropping and scuttled out the door again. Something fell in the garage (closed again) and the sliding door came up and banged down. No Mister though. We waited a couple minutes, cleaning up the last of the lunch specials for a bunch of campers from Idaho and then it was just the two of us.

We got spinny, plunking quarters in the box and dancing to Little Green Bag three times in a row. Dancing like a pair of banshees until another camper pulled in. I settled down and marched out to where the Wife was holed up in Cabin Three and told her through the door that Josie and I had to quit.

I heard the toilet flush. Quit! Flush! Like an exclamation mark. Spent half her life on the can I swear. She opened the door and glared at me.

"There's two weeks left in the season," she says in her

snappy boss voice. Her breath reeked of American cigarettes. Took me hours to air out a cabin after she'd holed up in it.

"Our Dad says you owe us 4 percent holiday pay," I say in my most polite and careful voice.

"But you girls didn't give us two weeks' notice," she says, folding her big huge arms over her big huge bazooms.

"Our Dad says it's the law and you didn't give us notice to work fifteen days straight either." Her mouth makes an O.

I take the plunge and make a decision for Josie and me. "If you give us our pay with the 4 percent, we won't charge overtime. Our Dad," I say, watching her squinty little eyes, using my most extremely polite voice now that I'm lying like a sidewalk, "Our Dad will come up tomorrow morning for us and I guess he'll talk to you about it if Mister isn't, ahh, around." I raise my eyebrows at her with this last bit.

That did it. She gave me a long, hard look and slammed the door in my face. I started running up to the kitchen, leaping from plank to wooden plank so I wouldn't sink into the mud lake between the cabins and the cafe.

There were some customers, the geologist guys from the Pink Mountain site, so I held it in until Josie took out their orders and came back into the kitchen. I retell the whole exchange with the Wife and we both get so excited our whispers shot up to squeaks and we tried to jump up and down without making noise, her in her wooden clogs and me in my gumboots.

Josie had big dark circles under her eyes and she'd lost fifteen pounds in a month and a half. She was more burnt out than me because short-order cooking and waitressing and night clean-up was all inside work, breathing a steady diet of grill grease and Pine-Sol. At least I could cart towels and linen in the fresh air between cabins. For the first few weeks there was a truck, the Alaska Highway Laundry Express, but then it folded and yours truly used an industrial washer and an outside clothes line about fifty yards long because their dryer had broken down. I liked doing laundry better than making beds and scrubbing toilets.

Outside the air smelled like spruce tea with the late summer mists hanging low and the roots dangling into the little river, steeping it a coppery brown colour. I could hear trucks downshifting miles and miles away, that throaty roar with a silent breath between gears. I stood up on the laundry line perch, singing my head off, pulling wet sheets, towels, pillow slips and kitchen cloths out of my basket and onto the line, or vice versa.

Back inside I tried to keep my mood light and summery, battling relief and giddiness and drawing a blank when it came to what to do next. I put the apron on to help Josie with night clean-up, strolling over to the juke-box to punch in some Creedence and Three Dog Night and Greenbaum's Little Green Bag, our theme song. The geologists chitchatted about rocks and bone hunters, one of them insisting that this place was smack in the middle of an ice-free corridor during the last glacier age. I poured their refills and kept my ears open because these guys always had the most interesting arguments. Then I heard the Wife giving Josie hell in the kitchen and so did the customers. I set the coffee pot down none too gently and marched back there, do or die.

Josie was looking white and shaky, holding a piece of

order pad with some figuring on it.

"You got your hopes up, girlie," says the Wife, standing with her feet splayed apart and her arms hoisted over her bazooms. She launched into a major bullying session with a tired little Grade Ten waitress. Honestly!

"And what's the problem here?" I snap out in a loud voice that shocks even me. Josie looks at me like we've got one last chance to live and hands over the slip of paper.

"I figured out what I've got coming to me and they won't give it," she says, close to crying.

Josie is very smart with math and so I (no genius) quickly check the end result. I pause just a few seconds. Not for nothing was Drama by best subject.

"Looks right to me," I say in my new loud way and stare the skinflint down. By this point I am amazing myself!

"I'm paying her for nine hours a day and that includes breaks and meals," she says, looking past me at the heads of the geologists who are lining up at the till. She starts to move but I jump in front of her, wanting witnesses in case Mister crawls out of his cubbyhole in the garage and things get really weird. The Wife is scary enough but I got to her earlier with the yak about our Dad and the law and I know it.

"This poor kid works more hours than the fourteen a day she's claiming," I say. "She's opened up and closed down this joint for half the summer and she better be paid for it." Then I step aside so she can face the geologists over the cash register. Let the old bag simper and coo about how they like her homemade soup now, the frigging hypocrite!

To make a long story shorter, we got our cheques that night without one word of thanks. By 7 a.m. the next morning we were facing a chilly north wind blowing gravel grit in our faces but in no time flat we were climbing into a big fuel tanker truck. Listening to Buck Owens and Merle Haggart on eight-track stereo. Homeward bound! It was a deluxe truck with a cabover for sleeping, tons of seat space, tinted windshield, little orange balls across the top that some truckers called Calgary willnots, don't ask me why, and swinging dice cubes in oversized green and white foam stuff. And then there were the naked ladies.

Once I saw them I couldn't stop staring at them out the corners of my eyes because they were cut up into parts and glued onto the dash and the middle of the horn and the ashtray. Mostly breasts, no heads or arms. I was glad the trucker, Al, he said he was, didn't want to talk much because I was sitting next to him. Josie always pulled the shy act when a ride slowed down for us and started whining for the outside seat. The music blared out of four speakers and Al tapped one finger on the wheel but he didn't keep time with the music, just kept the same beat. I had to make myself stop staring at that finger too.

I made myself look out at the scenery rolling by, the miles of stunted muskeg spruce and swamp tamarack giving way to taller spruce and pines and poplars. We passed a jack-knifed rig and a squashed station wagon, burnt to a grey crisp. Ugh. And there was a bunch of wild-looking horses in the ditch, at least twenty of them escaped from who knows where, up to their bellies in good grass, sly and happy-looking the way horses are when they're on the lam.

The sun was pouring into the cab even with the tinted windshield. Al put on sunglasses which made him look even more sinister with his pock-marked jowls and hooked nose, an overweight parrot in an Hawaiian shirt and dirty jeans. He asked Josie to reach into the glove compartment for his pills. "Gotta speed up my eyeballs," he said. "Hyuh, hyuh. Don't know your ass-pirin from your elbow, do ya, girlie?" Josie's giving him a confused, rabbity look because she can't get the lid of the flat black pillbox open. He asks her to fish two pills out for him. She still can't get the bloody little box open. I could scream.

The inside of the glove compartment is completely papered over with cut up women's crotch shots from magazines. You've got to understand that I'd never seen anything like this filth in my entire 17 years. This was beyond the regular girlie magazines in the drugstore in 1969 is what I'm saying. I know, it's everywhere today, the TV, everywhere. Makes me puke.

Josie broke a precious fingernail and finally opened the pillbox. Al gulped down two and sucked on an orange he kept up on the dash within reach.

He was really booting it, pedal to the metal, wanting to get to Edmonton by midnight. We roared through the village of Wonowon at eighty miles an hour. That's way over a hundred and twenty kliks to you. Too damn fast. Dogs and gas stations and trailer courts and little Indian kids on trikes blurred by us until a siren drowned out the Buckaroos.

Josie dug into my ribs. When Al cursed and started pumping the airbrakes and downshifting, she mouthed, "Out, out, out." Her face had gone white and every zit she'd ever had sprouted in purplish scar galaxies across her forehead and chin.

When the rig ground to a halt, we jumped out with the

big brown suitcase we shared and yelled our thanks. The young constable waved us on and motioned Al down from the truck for their little talk. Josie yanked at the suitcase and my arm at the same time and broke into a run. "Do you hafta pee or what's the panic?" I yelled. A red stock truck slowed down before I could even catch up to Josie and in it were two young guys with cowboy hats on. When I got closer I could see it was the Wayling brothers, rancher types from near the Blueberry Reserve. I didn't know them except to look at them and that was fine by me. Dark curly hair, cut short except for sideburns, grey eyes, gorgeous noses. They were, I told Josie later, like Zane Grey heroes minus their buckskin stallions.

We hopped in the truck and tried our damndest to get them to talk in full sentences for the fifty miles into town. Josie loosened them up with jokes about jogging on the highway to keep the pounds off and I, usually the yappier of us two, sat back and laughed and laughed. Josie was never funnier except they didn't get the one about hippies being living proof that cowboys screwed goats, which was just as well considering their occupation. I don't think they liked girls to swear or talk dirty and Josie figured that out in seconds. She hammed it up about disasters in the cafe kitchen when the only thing left to cook was freezer-burned hamburger and stale white bread. I bragged about her and Esther turning out fifteen pies at a time, cherry, apple, blueberry and lemon meringue. Josie flirted with them way worse than I ever did with the geologists. I had the outside seat too, did I mention that? Anyway, it was amazing what a summer of waitressing did for her confidence!

But once we got to Fort St. John, the brothers asked us to go cabareting and that's when they found out we weren't old enough to get in the bar and that was the end of that but it was fun while it lasted. They dropped us off at the end of our block like we asked because we didn't want our folks to see the truck and get ideas and besides, we had to talk. She told me there was a convex mirror on her side of the window and she'd looked into it and seen a pair of eyes between the curtains of the cabover, staring at her. That was just as we started to barrel through Wonowon. She stared back at the eyes, paralyzed with fright, and then the police siren saved the day. When I asked if it was men's eyes or women's eyes, she said she couldn't tell because of the warping of the mirror. Holy doodle. And here I was freaked out by the dirty magazine scissor work!

We tried not to dwell on it and we didn't tell our folks because the chances of us going further north to, say, Muncho Lake the next summer and earning really decent money would be shot down for sure. See? Not a brain in our heads — or more guts than brains is a better way of putting it.

Look, Carrie-Lynn, I'll spare you my grown-up jobs, 19 years and up, the classy night spots like the Oil King Cabaret where I pranced around in red polyester hotpants. Sure, laugh. Where I got bonked on the head by a flying beer glass for stepping between my friend Ella and a very hefty, very drunk woman who'd already yanked off Ella's frosted blonde short'n'curly wig. Poor Ella, standing there

SUMMER WAGES

in her red hotpants suit with bobby pins holding down her greasy brown hair. Don't laugh. A little giggle is all you're allowed. Now that's enough.

You could be a lifeguard. Or go down to the Tourist Information booth. You're smart, you're pretty, you've got a nice personality. Don't leave this godforsaken town until you're 18. Promise me that. You got the rest of your life.

Please?

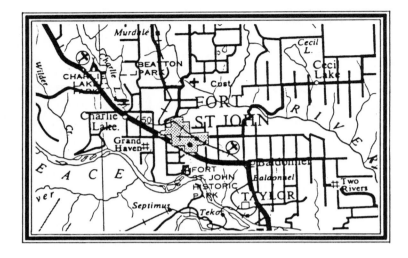

For the Daughters

Do the hard things at least once. Climb the farthest, highest branch of The Big Tree which has become the rite of passage in your neighbourhood. In your neck of the woods. Do this feat in memory of Amelia Earhart. Move toward bravery and the inner ringing bells of truth. Stick your neck out and breathe in the vapours of explorers gone before you.

Ride an old bay mare Comanche-style, off to one side so enemies won't see you. Won't hardly notice the bare foot hooked over the withers, half-hidden by a coarse black

FOR THE DAUGHTERS

mane. Practice going at a walk first. You are a rookie Comanche, after all.

Leave the bow and arrow behind. Concentrate on keeping the rope and yourself from hitting the ground, from corkscrewing down, down, the mane coming out in chunks, going under the hard, hard hooves of the old bay mare. Walk first. Then run. Skip the trot. No self-respecting Comanche would trot into battle. A trot will shake your brains out and cause many bruises on various body parts. Forget the trot.

Kick the mare into a rocking chair lope, kalump, kalump, like that. Get the hang of it, the lope, lean forward, take the biggest hunk of mane in your strongest hand, slide more than half your bum over to the same side as your strongest hand and bring your other knee up. Point your toe down and with your knee, sling, almost hook that knee over the high centre of the horse, slump down near the horse's shoulder, kalump, kalump, both hands buried in mane, and there!

The blood and guts of bravery begins with practice such as this, my daughter as yet unborn, of hard body and hard mind.

And when you're in town, maybe thirteen, in shorts and innocent and aware as well when the car slows down, up go your antennae, your built-in radar (ringing bells of truth) and when the man sez, Need a ride? You ask, Got lots of gas? They always say, Oh yeah! You bet! or words to that effect my dear one, my beautiful one, and then you say, Good! Step on it! and make a quick exit, slip into a front yard any front yard and go up the walk like you owned the place and make sure the car is gone. The message can take a while to sink in, but 32-year-old men cruising for

Grade 8 girls aren't exactly whole human beings to begin with. This is not just being saucy, although any evidence of calmness and wit is a turn-off. They want the giggle, the knock-kneed walk, the fluster and blush of the prey, but you are a Comanche. You have noticed the same grey Impala passing you twice. You have crossed to the other side of the highway. You will know how long it will take to run to some safe place, to wait to leap out of sight, to use the underground culvert to double-back, to climb into the sticky pine tree (who cares about some old clothes, honey), to run into the middle of the road to stop the potato chip truck going the other way, to jump up on its running board and yell, Go! Go! Don't stop till we get to the lights in town! For you are a Comanche and you will not be taken prisoner by anyone.

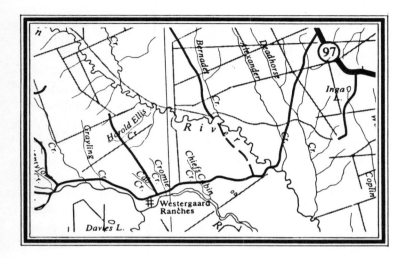

Bleeding Like a Goddess

"Uh huh," says Tess, studying the ramp and the fake Japanese bridge halfway down it and the tiers of seats, hundreds of seats, rising up on either side of the ramp.

They make their way to an exit and scuttle across the Pacific National Exhibition grounds, breathing in rancid popcorn and cotton candy and strange greasy smells, trotting because the rain had just started again.

Cheryl and Tess and twenty-six other farm girls do not intend to prance down the ramp during rehearsals or during the actual competition for Miss 4-H Fashion Queen.

They are ladylike. They have practised pivoting without throwing their hips out of joint. They do not take itty bitty steps resembling human poodles, or gigantic stomps like Parisienne models wearing mini skirts and bomber jackets tend to do. The farm girls pretty much glide around, unless they've inherited some bizarre family walk developed by tromping around after their fathers doing chores. Those unfortunate girls walk around like they've got gumboots on and the pavements of life have become just so much barnyard muck to cross.

This is Cheryl's last year in the North Peace Needle and Spool Club. She is modelling a gorgeous green evening gown that glints in the light. She is a very beautiful, some would say striking, girl of seventeen. Cheryl has been the most beautiful girl in the whole district since she was thirteen, surrounded by a gaggle of young girls who adore her blazing mop of auburn hair, her profile, her bustline, her slim brown arms, her soft, ladylike voice. Cheryl takes adoration in stride, accepting praise gracefully, as opposed to gratefully like our Tess.

Tess is one of her biggest fans, as a matter of fact, because Tess is short, almost plump, with poker-straight brown hair and a nice enough face but nothing outstanding. Cheryl has boys lined up for years with crushes on her, and even some men just waiting for her to get older. Tess has been going steady with a nice farm boy for two years and she can't quite put a finger on it yet, but she's bored.

Tess has made a dark red velvet semi-formal and her speech is polished and gleaming. She could say it backwards in her sleep. Two and a half minutes of spritely commentary on this dress of hers: why she chose the fabric, why the Empire waistline flatters her figure, the trouble she took with seam finishes, the lapped zipper, the clever little puffed sleeves, and, of course, her accessories, and a list of all the places and occasions she intends to appear in this dazzling little dress. Tess loves this dress and gets into it with careful little wiggles, smoothing the luxurious velvet with the back of her hands so her palms won't sweat all over it and stain it.

The preliminary modelling sessions go smoothly for both of them. They have each appeared as finalists, the top ten models, before, so their worst fears and stagefright are long gone. Still, Tess gets a small case of the jitters just before she's announced to go on.

"What's the worst thing that can happen?" asks Cheryl.

"I could fall on my face."

"But you won't."

"I could forget my speech."

"But you won't."

And she doesn't, of course. She glides down the ramp, pauses at the rise of the fake Japanese bridge, smiles as if she's just spotted Sam at the front door with a corsage in his hand, continues to glide to the T-junction of the ramp, pivots with smooth grace and veers left, pauses, smiles as if she's just thanked Sam for the orchid, pivots and veers left to the end of the T, keeps smiling at all the sweet things Sam is saying, pivots and returns to the main ramp, crosses the bridge with toes pointed in the same direction at a three-quarter angle to the wretched slope of it, then glides to the microphone at centre stage. By this time Tess is radiant. Her speech is half over before she knows it. She pauses, regains her focus, continues with more meaning compressed into the mundane words.

Rayon velvet. Black suede shoes with bows on the toes.

Clutch purse to match. Wrist-length transparent black gloves. Matching red velvet hair band. Perfect for Christmas parties!

Tess finishes and flashes another happy grin at the crowd, which she pictures as her friends all crowded into the washroom next to the gym. Putting on more make-up, helping each other with hair-dos, gossiping like crazy about how the dance is going. Sam is there too, loyal Sam, thoughtful Sam who will propose to her on graduation night and whose heart she will break because she doesn't ever want to get married and be called Mother by her husband. She's been trying to give back his big lumpy ring for a year and a half, but she can't find the words, make the right speech. He is just too nice, and she feels awful about all of it. The applause is enthusiastic and Tess snaps back into focus as she exits.

The scene backstage is controlled nervous energy. Girls waiting to go on are silently mouthing their speeches, waving their hands in practised gestures. They pace in tiny steps so as not to annoy anyone else. There isn't much room. Girls who've finished their routines strip off, hang up their precious outfits, protect them with a double layer of dry-cleaning bags, and head for the washroom to take off make-up. And collapse in a ladylike sort of way.

There are no mothers allowed backstage. In fact, not very many mothers are even in the audience. Cheryl and Tess have mothers eight hundred miles away which is just as well. Things are tense enough without seeing those familiar glasses gleaming in the crowd, lips tightly stretched over their teeth, waiting for the first mistake.

"I goofed my speech," says Cheryl in the washroom.

"No way!" Tess leaps to her defense.

BLEEDING LIKE A GODDESS

"Yep. It's the part about the placket, the Princess lines and the *peau de soie* fabric. There's too many p's too close together, and I told my mother that a hundred times, but she said it would help me remember it better! God!"

Cheryl is peeved, but Tess hands her a wintergreen Lifesaver. Then they hear the applause for the last contestant. They jump into their jeans and make their way to the sidelines where everyone else is waiting.

A big blonde girl is in tears, still wearing her ice blue formal and holding a silver sandal with a heel ripped off. Tess hears her mumble "damn bridge" to the girl next to her who shushes her up and rolls her eyes. Such bad luck may be catching, like a virus, and sympathy is in short supply.

The fashion show moderator reads the judges' list of finalists from the show, with the Grand Finale to begin at two o'clock the next day. Cheryl and Tess both make the list and start to move away, but Tess stops, points to the ramp and tugs at Cheryl's arm.

"You know, I've always looked at models like they were goddesses or something. I can't believe I'm here!"

Cheryl just smiles her secretive little smile at this outburst from Tess.

The Grand Finale clicks along with semi-professional flair. The Muzak is cheerful and anonymous, easy to walk to. Cheryl is the picture of grace, getting smatterings of applause as she pivots. Tess stands immediately behind her backstage, all ears. Her speech seems to take forever. She is labouring over the froth of words. She says "pracket" instead of "placket." "Princer" instead of "princess." "Bridesmad" for "bridesmaid." Finally, she barrels through the exit and grabs Tess' free hand.

CAROLINE WOODWARD

"Do it for our club!" she implores.

Tess marches out, remembering yesterday's substitution of Sam, solid, dependable Sam and her high school friends and smiling, smiling, remembering the hours spent on aprons, skirts, needlecases, bedsocks, housecoats, interminable samples for record books, wool suits, semiformals and finally, formals. Smile, smile, smile! She invests every word of her speech with significance. Tess is realizing, and not for the first time, that she loves being on stage even to confide her zipper technique to hundreds of strangers. Tess has learned to keep her joy a secret while making sure she is competent beyond a shadow of a doubt, and damn well deserves to be up there on that stage.

It takes a long time for the judges to come to a conclusion, or so it seems to the ten finalists who have kept their outfits on, in readiness for the final parade or, better yet, a dash for the roses, the tiara, the gold sash proclaiming MISS 4-H FASHION QUEEN.

In third place is a brunette from Enderby wearing a sophisticated evening gown with matching gloves up to her biceps. Cheryl is the second runner-up. She hugs Tess and they are both stunned. She should have been first, and they both think it without saying it. Neither one can smile. They open their mouths and hang on to each others forearms. But Cheryl gets a marvelous long bout of applause as she accepts her flowers. Miss 4-H Fashion Queen 1969 is Tess. That's what the disembodied voice at the microphone has announced. She is stunned twice over. Someone gives her a little push and she collects her wits, clutches her little black velvet purse, and walks to where they are all waiting.

BLEEDING LIKE A GODDESS

Roses, sash, tiara, princesses, the works. Kiss, kiss.
Flashbulbs pop away. Smile, smile, her face will break,
smile some more.
"Now you're one of the goddesses," whispers Cheryl
and smiles that knowing little smile.
"But you are, *you* are!" blurts out Tess and starts to cry
like all Queens seem to do, suffering the acute agony of
actually getting what their most secret heart wants, which
means making other hearts bleed in grief, albeit girlish
grief, the kind that lasts a lifetime.

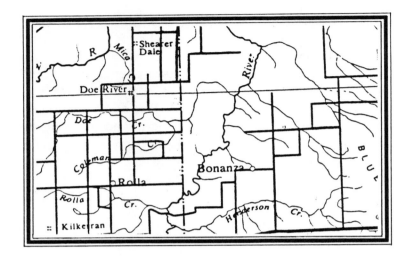

Renegade Hens

Renegade Hen lurks in the tree that no hens are supposed to fly up to. Renegade is mostly Leghorn—lean, mean and wild-eyed. The rest are inside the chicken house, counting all their eggs, eating till their gizzards pop, romancing the tired old rooster. Their plump red hulks are all cozied up on the roosts.

But she, the runaway, the renegade, is not afraid of the dark. She hangs on, a little unsteadily it's true, to the poplar branch twelve feet up and makes a tiny angry bubbling noise back in her throat.

RENEGADE HENS

Her eggs are small and extremely white. She's the harlot of the chicken world. She won't go near the regular egg boxes inside the house to lay any of her precious farm fresh ova. This one squats in the furthest corner under the roosts. Or out behind the woodpile. Under the barn ramp. In the tool box of the old John Deere.

She waits. The moon rises. A woman carries a full pail of milk from the barn to the house. Lights go on automatically in the barnyard, the better to see bears, anything with rabies, or, God forbid, flames. Lights go off in the chicken world. Renegade Hen sighs, almost happy, undetected on the poplar branch and sleeps the sleep of the unrepentant.

□   □   □

Myrtle the Cowgirl turns on the old radio in the barn. It's a proven fact that cows produce more milk to music. Not heavy metal, mind you, more like Chopin. Myrtle's cows do fine with vintage country: Kitty Wells, Bob Wills, Tennessee Ernie Ford, and best of all, Patsy Cline. It's no coincidence that milking time is 8 o'clock sharp, just like CJDC's Classic Country Hour.

Myrtle grabs the rickety milking stool, the shining galvanized pail and plops herself down next to the sweet-faced Jersey. Kitty croons and wails it like it really is about honkytonk angels and who created them in the first place. Myrtle lays her head in the long warm V-shaped hollow in Butterfield Mae's flanks and sings along.

The double streams of milk foam in the pail and Myrtle floats away. Up and away from her messy housebound world with five healthy, yammering kids, a skinny little husband who can't get enough of her and the fifty extra pounds she's gained, ten pounds per baby, weighing her

CAROLINE WOODWARD

down, making her wheeze. She rises in a glittering cowgirl sateen shirt and tight white jeans with boots over top and a white hat on her curls, looking remarkably like Jessica Lange. This is why Myrtle won't teach the oldest one to milk.

Myrtle comes back to the house at dusk, singing softly to herself, and starts up a fine-tuned humming and purring at the cream separator in the pantry, one spout skimmed milk, the other a fine cream, Myrtle, still smiling, still glowing.

□   □   □

Down the road half a mile, Myrna rolls her twenty-fifth cigarette and stacks it with the others in a black velvet case. It snaps shut with a solid metallic click. On Friday she is going to the Dawson Creek Hospital to have her gall bladder yanked out. Bad enough she's got diabetes and poor circulation.

"Life's a bitch and then you die" is what Myrna has tacked up on the wall in her sewing room. Myrna is used to feeling rotten, and she says so at least three times a day. Nobody listens. Her boys are good for nothing except rolling cars and getting very young girls knocked up. She rents the land out to a neighbour and gets by, just barely, she tells the boys, who want their Dad's money for this or that.

Five years earlier her husband took out a bunch of insurance on himself in February and rolled the tractor on himself in May. Myrna has gone to Reno on package tours twice a year ever since, but life is no longer sweet no matter how many trips she takes. New chesterfield and drapes be damned. "To hell with it all," says Myrna out

loud, smacking her TV wand which doesn't work worth
a crap unless it's pointed right at the set. She doesn't want
the news. She wants a half-decent movie, that's why she
got that satellite dish monstrosity in the first place. Myrna
often stays up all night, smoking and jumping from
channel to channel.

□   □   □

Sometime around daylight, the newest victim huddles
under the roosts where she spent the night. Too tired to
fly up and claim her rightful place as a producer, a
reliable layer of brown eggs in her day. Feathers waft
off her back and looking closer, advancing, we see the
bald, scabby patches. Exciting.

An experimental peck by our leader. She jerks back a
little. A squeak. Another peck. A half-hearted defense.
Take a couple swipes just below the neck, someone
hisses. There, where it joins the back. Lots of bald surface. There. And there.

The chicken house fills with a scuttling, rustling noise
and then the soft footfalls of twenty pairs of chicken
claws marching over wood shavings and shit and silent
downy feathers. Toward the undersized one in the
corner, weeping. Trying to have a heart attack to be
done with it quickly. Instead of bleeding to death with
everyone else getting drunk on her blood. Praying also
for a concussion. A good sharp peck on the skull and
nothing.

□   □   □

At the next house on Haliburton Road with the lights
off by nine-thirty, summer and winter, is Maggie Morris

and her oddball friend in the little trailer, the one who changes her name about once a year. Maretta Dawn Giddings aka Aurora Dawn Giddings aka Melinda Hope Giddings and on and on for about nine different names. This boggles the mind of the community at large.

Maggie is a strange, mean hermit with a permanent scowl on her face as far as the rest of Haliburton Road is concerned so Maretta's name-changing antics are a pleasant enough diversion. As are her flouncy Southern belle clothes and the bright yellow Japanese jeep she drives like a bat out of hell down Haliburton Road.

People can't figure out what she's doing at Maggie's place for going on three years now. Maggie's folks died in a smash-up between their grain truck and a P.G.E. freight train when she was seventeen. Maggie ran her own brother off the place the day she turned twenty-one, and he was one year older. He always bounced in and out of jail, starting young. People say he beat her up and worse. Maggie took to wearing overalls and gum-boots and her father's old shirts. Anybody who didn't have business being on her place got shown the gate, pronto. Except Maretta of course.

□   □   □

At the Co-op Myrtle Owens told Myrna Jenkins that she'd seen Maggie and Maretta walking back from the river breaks with a milk pail full of saskatoons between them, walking and laughing like a pair of school girls. Myrna sniffed and looked sideways.

"If you can't say anything nice, don't say anything at all," she said and smirked in that sneaky way of hers. Myrtle was truly bewildered.

RENEGADE HENS

"But it *was* nice to see Maggie laughing, is all. Enjoying herself, having fun with company. Nothing wrong with that, is there, Myrna?"

Myrna shrugged her leathery little shoulders and Myrtle felt herself getting into a huff and decided to finish her shopping and get on home.

□   □   □

Renegade Hen will be stringy and tough. The rest leave her alone. A hen hierarchy depends on size, weight, general alertness and an undefinable streak of meanness. The ability to lunge at somebody else's eyes. The urge to flaunt a wingspan quicker than anybody else. To knock somebody off balance for the sheer pleasure of it. You can watch it operate at the half-tires filled with grain and water and oyster shell. There'll be a couple hogs. Top hens. Queen bees, all the same diff. Same goes for the laying boxes. The Top Hen picks the very first box so everyone else has to walk further down to find an empty one and work away.

□   □   □

Maggie Morris used to get migraines so bad she'd crawl into the pantry where it was coolest and lay down on a cot she kept there for just that purpose. Sometimes they lasted three days. She hasn't had a bad one for about three years. She still jams a heavy-bladed knife into both doors at night and puts the German Shepherd on the long line between the house and the trailer porch. She keeps the old duck gun, a shotgun, in her bedroom. Just in case.

□   □   □

CAROLINE WOODWARD

Renegade Hen will end up as stew, or coyote finger food. She will have the last laugh, if anyone can catch her at all. This bird can *fly*.

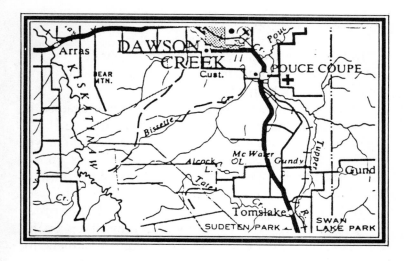

Sliding Home

Elly hangs upside down, folded at the waist, arms dangling several inches above the carpet. Every muscle group and connecting tendon in her body aches. Both knees quiver beneath the sweatpants. Raggedy Elly.

"Hal," she says, looking at his upside-down face. "Hal, I'm incredibly stiff. I can't remember the last time I felt this way." She sways gingerly from side to side, grunting softly. "Rigor mortis from the knees down."

He rolls over and talks into the pillow. "Time for the twilight league, Elly, old gal. Let's face it, even latent jocks have to retire gracefully."

A wheezy chuckle. Asthma, she notes.

"Hal, I just need a massage. Empathetic hands."

"Hint, hint. Doesn't that coach give you older types some time to catch up on conditioning?"

She snorts, stands up too quickly, and leans against the dresser. "The old eye-hand coordination is still intact!" An argyle sock connects with his head. "I'm coping quite well with the phys-ed teachers and childless joggers on our team. And not doing too badly for someone in the prime of life. Don't get ageist on me, punk!"

"Well, as long as you don't end up on crutches or smash the dental work," he says, propping himself up on his elbows. "You haven't done anything remotely athletic for years and you could injure yourself, is all I'm saying."

"Remotely athletic? What do you call raising three kids and chasing after hundreds of clients? Nice talk, Mortimer!" Another sock skims the top of his hair, rebounds off the headboard and flops neatly on his head. He snatches if off while she shrieks with glee. An argyle toupee.

"Hey, cut it out! And quit calling me Mortimer."

"Okay, Mort. I'm off." Smooch. "See ya later, city boy. I've got a breakfast meeting lined up with the summer students."

Halfway out the front door she yells, "We're playing the Esso Gaslighters at home tonight if you want to watch."

□   □   □

Elly says to the summer students in the cafeteria that softball is her latest therapy. They look amused, if not convinced.

SLIDING HOME

"Lookit," Elly leans over the table, "after a day of active listening and crisis intervention, there's something to be said for picking up a silver Louisville Slugger and whalloping a ball. Stare it down all the way from the pitcher's knuckles to the plate. Focus! Judgment! Fair or foul. Bash it to hellangone!"

They stare at her with uncertain smiles on their faces. She tries again.

"How can you stay in knots about bureaucrats and cutbacks and life in general when you're running sideways and backwards, squinting into the sun, trying to catch a high infield fly?"

The student child-care worker smiles then, for the first time since breakfast, an honest grin.

"I swim laps," she allows. Susan is her name.

"I read P.D. James and dance," says Julie from up north.

□   □   □

On the homefront, Elly finds herself winging clothes into the washer and dryer at ten paces. Hal is still working on the massive stone wall around the yard and she practises shotputting the abundant supply of rocks. He learns to respond to "Waddaya say, hey!" by sticking out his palms so she can slap them one after the other and then present her own. This signifies any job well done, as in weeding the entire garden or painting the shed.

"Well, waddaya say, hey?"

Whap, whap. Whop, whop.

□   □   □

The Pouce Coupe Drycleaners Ladies Softball Team, renamed the Clean Machine by Elly, practises twice a week.

Her station wagon reliably transports women of all shapes and sizes, plus water coolers, dry ice packs and the team equipment bag. Merv from the Liquor Store coaches them well and brings the beer. Elly notices Merv blossoming in his coaching role as the season progresses. "Go for it!" he yells and they do. He buys a stopwatch for running drills and wields it proudly. He's hoarse after games, the result of bellowing encouragement at the Clean Machine.

"Nice bum, eh?" says Joannie in a wicked whisper from the corner of her mouth during a practise. Merv is bending over the backcatcher who has caught one of Joannie's wilder pitches in the gut. Elly and Joannie turn away from the scene of the accident, stifling giggles. Girl talk. Teen queens rule. Joannie is thirty-three and Elly is forty-four.

□ □ □

Think then throw. Call the ball! Watch home. Cover each other. Block the grounders. Bunt, spring, slide.

They watch Merv for batting signals. A tug on his hat brim means hit the first pitch and boot it quick for first base. A casual slap on the hip means bunt. Arms folded across his chest indicates letting the next pitch go by. If this strategy works, the runner on first can steal second while a runner on third noisily fakes a run home.

He is teased unmercifully by his beer store buddies for coaching women's softball but the Clean Machine is in second place by mid-July and steadily improving.

After the second tournament of the season, Elly comes into the kitchen at a fast clip. Hal is drying dishes. She grabs him around the waist and starts to squeeze.

SLIDING HOME

"Hold it, Elly! I've got a plate here!"

"Oops, sorry. But we won! Five games straight!" She holds out her palms.

He picks up his drink and surveys a short, sweating woman with beer breath. His wife. Elly.

"Didn't I tell you, folks? That this team could only improve? And we're seeing it now, seeing it now." He does a credible Howard Cosell.

Elly continues unabated. "You should have seen us tonight! It wasn't like that game you saw in June, I mean we were making plays like..."

"Okay, okay. You were great, Elly, I'm sure." He raises the rum and Coke.

"That's not what I mean," she says, "it's not just me, everybody..."

The bottom of his glass bumps against her nose.

"Well, here's to everybody then," he says, setting the drink down and turning back to the dishes.

The bump on the bridge of her nose stings. Off-base move, she goes to say but stops because her eyes are watering. She decides to take a shower.

□ □ □

In the bedroom she stretches for ten minutes, using the wall to brace herself. He reads the condensed copy of the Applebert Report. The reading lamp goes off as she slides onto the undulating surface of the Aqua-Dream Queen.

"Hal? Is something up?"

"No. Oh, Katie phoned from UBC today. She'll need about five hundred bucks from us by September."

"That's not too bad. How is she? How did she sound?"

"Alright, I guess. In a big rush, as usual."

"Mmmm. Geoff and Greg won't need more than that with their fire fighting work paying so well, which is too bad for the trees, but anyway, maybe we can take a little holiday, you and me, eh? I've got a bundle of stats owing."

"Oh, sure. On your money, it'll have to be. Just like the extra university money for the kids. The last thing I need is a holiday! I don't know what you think I do all day!"

"Look, Hal, let's talk. Things aren't great with us. I know it. Your work..."

"I'm exhausted, Elly. Beat. Four days straight in Victoria is enough to wear anyone out."

"But we haven't made love for at least a month, haven't gone out, you wouldn't go to dinner at Ron and Surinder's even!"

"Just stop it! I don't need this Elly."

"Whatsamatter? You don't need the facts, the observable facts you talk about, or you don't need to make love?"

"I just don't need to be hassled about it now. I'm tired, Elly, I have to get some sleep."

"I'm sorry," she says to the back of his neck, kissing it. Nuzzling his shoulder and tucking herself into the long curve of his body.

"Elly, you're too hot right next to me," he says, moving over.

A new series of rubberized waves beneath them makes her suddenly nauseous. She rolls off the bed and gropes her way to the open window.

Maybe it's a matter of timing with us, she thinks. Another cruel joke courtesy of Ma Nature on the job market in this damn province. "All the young guys with their MBA's get the contracts," he'd told her yesterday at breakfast, or maybe it was the day before. "Fifteen years of experience and a 1966 BA in Art History don't impress anyone uptown," he'd said. Bitter again. Moving from the city to Pouce Coupe was great for her, on the other hand. A promotion. This nice old house. Her favourite kind of small community and good people at work too. Instead of having freelance contracts fall through and plans go awry, she's hitting her stride, booming along like never before. Just that afternoon Merv beamed at her, softly punching her shoulder. "Wayta hustle around those bases, Elly!" She's the third fastest runner on the team now. And she'd grinned back until he blushed and turned away, yelling the next runner home.

She leans against the windowsill, shaking her head. If anyone is going to have a fling, it'll be Hal. She almost says it out loud. She stands up straight, knocking her head on the curtain rod. Classic textbook stuff, she thinks, straightening the collapsed rod. Her hands shake and the fingers tremble of their own accord. The stuff she presumes to counsel other adults about. Communication. Commitment. Responsibility. Rituals. Mid-life career and relationship crises. Out-of-sync sexual energy. Letting go. Foul play. Foreplay. Fair play. Hah, hah, very funny, Elly.

□ □ □

Elly plays shortstop, the hot spot. She thrives on it, keeps up a steady stream of chatter, and calls the plays for the infield. Big Cooper glove. The Cooper Scooper. She springs around in new black and white-striped cleats. They are marketed as boys' soccer shoes, but they suit softball and Elly admirably. The Clean Machine players wear snazzy orange and white uniforms, cleaned weekly by their sponsor.

CAROLINE WOODWARD

"C'mon now, Joannie, hum it on in there like you can now!"

Joannie is easily one-half the team. A tall gangling blonde who pitches best when she's furious. The sight of a batter is enough to get her jaws working savagely on a wad of sugarless gum.

"Okay! Umchuck now, Big, Chucker!"

"You're lean, you're mean, you got 'er swingin' now, Joannie!"

The Clean Machine is a vocal, assertive bunch, especially when they're winning.

"Airmail it to China, baby!"

"Wayta mix 'em up now. It's two for you, two for you."

"Like you can, Jan, like you can."

"Here we go now, one two three, now, let's get tight out here!"

□   □   □

Elly gets a little literary on the diamond for the benefit of her infield colleagues and to wear off the nervous tide of adrenalin welling up inside her while she waits. She chants in a mullah's high voice.

"Lo! The sizzle of a vicious line drive between third and short! The sheer poetry of a double-play. La-dee-dah! The sweet bruising glory, ladies and ladies, bruising glory of sliding home safe!"

Then she emulates her favourite uncle, Albert the auctioneer. "Hustle for it oh yeah scoop it and to first! Yeehaw! Sold! And fire it home!...Cover, cover, great!... and back to Joannie for some wing-ding pitchin' oh yeah it's a fine line. Wooooeee! It's fair...MINE!" as she scrambles under the pop flies and pounces on the shinbone killers bouncing crazily toward her.

The last game of the season begins on the Pouce Coupe diamond in 100 percent humidity under a rumbling black sky. The Clean Machine versus the Prince George B Division Champs. Huge, serious types with intimidating uniforms.

"I bet they're all on steroids," Elly hisses as she runs past Joannie. But Joannie is working on replacing her initial fearful choke with a grim fury and dusty palms.

Things start coming apart in the bottom of the sixth. Clean Machine fielders collide. Joannie starts pitching wild. Easy pop flies are fumbled and dropped. Green and black uniforms race around the bases, racking up seven runs before retiring to the field. Elly's glove rattles a fly ball so much she nearly loses it but her throw to first is fast and snappy. The Clean Machine dogtrots in to begin a salvage operation at bat.

The first two up go out on an easy left field fly and a mis-aligned bunt right to the hulking green pitcher. Elly steps up and assumes her most menacing stance at home plate.

Low ball coming.

She thinks she hears Merv yell, "Take it, Elly!"

Too late. She swings viciously and scrambles down the baseline, seeing the ball arc over the right fielder. She lengthens her stride to catch the corner of the bag and races for second. Pulled 'em out of position, she thinks, as she rounds the second base bag for third. They're used to me hitting low in left field. Pounding feet, pounding heart. Merv is jumping up and down at third.

"Go home, Elly, go home!" he hollers.

She charges. Doing good turns on the bases is her forte. The catcher stretches out. The ball sinking into her glove. Elly hurtles for home plate, one soccer shoe defiantly high. Landing heavily on her right leg instead of on her ass.

"You're out!" yells the ump.

"Oh shit," groans Elly, unheard amid the outraged hub-bub from the sidelines of the Clean Machine contingent. She spits dust and hauls herself up from the ground. Her first leg is numb from the knee up.

She goes home to soak in a hot bath before the League Banquet. Reliving the last play amid sea-green bubbles. Marvelling at the massive bruise saddle-bag on her upper right thigh. She surveys the damage, the season's collage of lumps and bruises on her feet and legs. Two blackening toenails. It hurts to use the loofah. But they're strong, muscled legs, she affirms silently, rinsing off.

"Strong back, heavy haunches. A real farm gal," she says out loud. Uncle Albert praising a feisty Percheron mare.

Then downstairs with Hal.

"C'mon, Hal, it'll be fun!" Entreaty. "You'll have a good time without me." Statement. A no go.

One knee bumps against the side of the armchair and he plops himself down heavily.

"You always have a good time, doncha Elly?" He extends a hand to the rack of coasters on the coffee table.

Bad timing. Lousy timing. Another consulting bid down the drain this afternoon. A large Coke, half a bottle of white rum, and an empty ice-cube tray in the kitchen.

"We could dance tonight!" She twirls in her bright yellow dress.

"Nice outfit. Makes you look slim." He settles back in the chair, glass raised in a toast, eyes wavering somewhere over her left shoulder.

SLIDING HOME

"Well, I have lost twelve pounds this summer! I am...
going now," she says and turns, not looking back. Crying
outside in the old Rambler. Cranking the radio up as loudly
as she can stand it.

"Diamonds are a girl's...diamonds are a girl's...yeah,
diamonds are a girl's best friend," she hollers along with
the Broadway musical voices, all the way into town. When
she stops to park the station wagon, she hears reggae
music pounding through the walls of the Legion Hall.

"Lookin' good, Elly," says Joannie at the door. "Where's
Hal?"

"At home. Watching a video. Patton. If you can fathom
that!"

"You need a beer," observes Joannie.

Elly steps into the hall. There are at least a hundred
players, all tarted up in fancy dress knickers, off-the-
shoulder dresses, leather, georgette, raw silk, a rainbow of
eyeshadows, glittering fingernails and fragrant clouds of
competing colognes and deodorants. Eau de ninth inning,
sniffs Elly appreciatively. Evening in Downtown Pouce
Coupe, indeed!

The teams, their coaches and the supporting cast of
umps, sponsors, boyfriends, girlfriends and husbands
congregate around the smorgasbord table and the bar. Elly
tucks into corn on the cob, salads and cold cuts heaped on
a Chinet plate.

The sound system starts crackling and sputtering. Merv,
almost dapper in a suit, holds a beer in one hand and a
microphone in the other. He introduces the coaches from
the other teams and thanks the Women's Institute for
catering.

Beginning with the bottom of the league team and

CAROLINE WOODWARD

moving up to the tournament winners, the coaches and sponsors make their presentations. Merv takes up the microphone last. The Clean Machine lets out one long, loud wolf whistle in unison. He blushes right on cue and the unruly bunch clap and whistle encouragement.

One of the social work summer students, Julie, a consistent centre fielder and heavy hitter from Fort St. John, gets the Rookie of the Year award to wild applause. Their backcatcher, Evie, pressed into that crucial position this season, gets Most Improved Player. She also gets a pair of oversize sunglasses to hide black eyes (three this season). The Most Valuable Player trophy, a gorgeous gold-coloured statuette dropping a bat and heading for first, goes to Elly, amid whistles, stomping, yahooing and much clinking of beer bottles at the Clean Machine table.

Merv shakes her hand and then leans over quickly, his lips brushing her ear. Tiny chills.

"Elly, your slip is showing!" he whispers urgently.

She jerks her head back and hears the raucous hooting from far away. He looks at her seriously, very wholesomely.

"It is. Sorry, honest." He still shakes her hand. She stands, nodding and smiling, holding the trophy upside down. It takes forever to walk back to the table.

"We're lean, we're mean, we're the Clean Machine," they chant, happily regressing to junior high.

She walks home singing, drunk with glory and several more beer than she is used to.

I've drunk more than three
And I'm lookin' for sailors
Won't somebody tell me
Where's the damn sea.

SLIDING HOME

"Hey, Hal!" she bellows in the porch. "Look what I got!" She leaps into the living room and brandishes the MVP golden girl.

He is asleep on the couch. Soldiers clash silently on the screen. She sees, for the first time, that his curly hair is thinning on top. One leg dangles at an angle off the couch. His hands are cupped over his crotch.

She puts the golden girl on top of the TV beside the soapstone walrus, yanks off her slip, hangs it off a tusk and walks over to the couch.

"Hal," she whispers, lurching over his right ear, "Hal?"

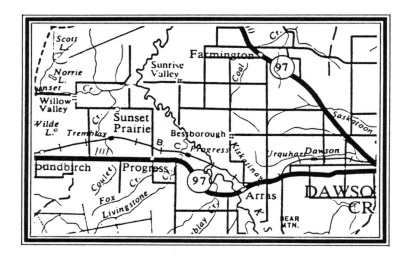

Henriksen's Urn

There is calm tonight. The air is like hand lotion, light and wet, rosewater and glycerin. But I should have brought my winter coat, after all. The North Atlantic is still north in June. Yet in two days, maybe less, we'll see the coast.

"No! This is final!" you bellowed and slammed your fist on my table.

That was in March. There was still time to make bookings for the children. It wasn't like it was your money, Gunnar. You never got over the money from my family. A wife with money in the Dawson Creek bank. God knows how you tried to get it out of me.

HENRIKSEN'S URN

I wanted the children with me. Right up to the end, I kept after you about them. Oma wants to see them, I said over and over again, and she isn't long for this world. Have you no heart, Gunnar? No.

You must have the boys to put the crop in and Sonja to cook. I could go alone to the Old Country you said. You start out quiet and end up roaring, big veins popping in your neck.

More land you wanted, telling me about this quarter or that section, not looking me in the eye, just soft talk till I wanted to pour hot porridge down your throat.

You were seeding wheat the day I got the envelope all bordered in black. Oma died without seeing the children or me again, and I will never forget that or forgive anything.

"A man has to eat around here," you said the day after. Slamming the doors of the kitchen cupboards. So I got up and made food. I watched you stuffing your mouth with fried pork, gravy slopping on your beard. Wolfing down potatoes and mashed turnips after the meat. I made a quart sealer of tea with two tablespoons of sugar, and meat sandwiches and butter cake for Sonja to pack out to the field after school for your afternoon tea. Eat, I said to myself that day, eat, choke on it, eat some more! I knew that day I would leave. Finally. I had to leave.

You never thought I would. The pawing in bed, the soft voice, the days of sulking did not fool me. You thought I would spend my money on your big dreams for land and forget about seeing my family overseas. Talk of land could make you slobber like a dog. But not me. Alice Sorenson did not come down with yesterday's rain, oh no!

But all last summer I prayed for rain. I packed water from the scoop-out every evening to my poor suffering

CAROLINE WOODWARD

garden. You walked the fields and watched the crop turn yellow and the first milk kernels shrivel. You wanted the money to seed with barley then. Plough under the wheat and try barley to beat the frost, you said. With my money. No, I said. I'd bought the tickets by then and you still didn't believe me. You searched for them too, I know. In the kitchen drawers. In the trunk. Through my old letters. No rain. And then the morning of the fourteenth of August, we wake up to a foot of snow, my dahlias poking out of a high.drift against the house. All was still and silent and strange, the animals, the birds, the wind.

You hitched the mare and the two-year-old colt to the Democrat and went to town. I couldn't say anything then. And I couldn't blame you for wanting a drop. To sit with the other farmers in the Fort Hotel. Your face was so grey and terrible. Even the children spoke in whispers. The earliest snow in memory. A white world except for the shadows left by the wheels and hooves.

They brought you home long after dark, your chest kicked in and arms pulled out of their sockets. Dead and stinking of beer and something else. Runaway team, they said. Down by the river. The colt had welts all over his back. Only green-broke. Not used to snow or the bridge or beatings.

And this is final too, Gunnar Henriksen. Ashes. Just this small handful of you. Floating now on the white furrows behind this boat, with seagulls instead of crows shrieking and greedy overhead. I am doing the seeding now, one handful at a time, Gunnar. Almost done ploughing through the ocean. Tomorrow we step off the S. S. Gripsholm in Gothenburg. Already I can smell the land. Pine trees and old leaves coming through the salt. You would like this, yes?

O, Gunnar, yes.

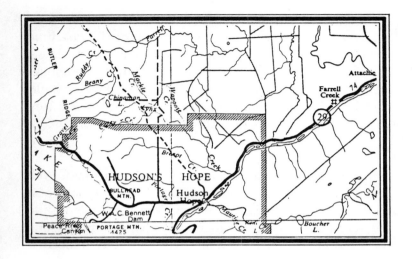

Reuben

(1940 — ?)

I'm going to fix the carb once and for all, dammit to hell.
Truck's eight months old. Figure it's a lemon part, minor.
Not worth the guarantee, warranty, whatever. Twice I've
cleaned it, adjusted the damn thing. Shouldn't need a
whole new kit, for chrissakes! My day off, got better things
to do. Huh? Who...o...?

MISSING: One new red 1968 Ford pickup. Black vinyl interior.
B.C. licence plates BOX 1E8. Tool-box mounted in truck box,
painted black, locked. Two-gun rack mounted on inside of
cab: .22 and shotgun.

I could make it into town, get down to Acklands for a kit, get back here before noon if the rides are good. Lotsa time, lotsa time. Better start hitching outside of camp, might see somebody I know going in, flag 'em down. Done enough favours myself. Maybe I oughta knock on Eddy's trailer first. Hey, Ed! Car's out here. Well, lights are on. Ed! Hey, ya gotta floozy in there or what? Ed! Move your ass!

May as well have a little look in, Ed won't mind. Well! Jeez Murphy! Some woman's moved *in* by the looks of it, all cleaned up, appliances to beat the band, some little kid's stuff all in the corner there...I better get my face outa the window and have me a talk with old Eddy tomorrow! Never said a word to any of his buds about this little set-up.

Male Caucasion. 5' 10''. 190 lbs. Eyes blue. Hair dark blonde. Complexion fair. No tattoos or scars. Last seen wearing red windbreaker, Cat hat, Lee jeans, grey sweatshirt, Tony Lama boots.

Here we go! Brand new car, stick the old mitt out, must be some guy from the job. Hey! Guy's goin' like a bat outa hell, don't have the time of day for me, eh? I'd like to know where the hell he works. Snot-nosed engineer maybe. Heavy equipment operator's too grubby for 'em, as if they could do bugger-all without us!

Now, here's more like it. Old Mennonite truck by the looks of it. Damn lucky they're not a tractor-driving bunch. Look at 'em, won't even look straight at me but they've slowed down nicely. I'll just hop in the back here,

thanks eh! Jeez! Whoops, watch my language, sorry, but I
barely got both boots in before ya took off again!
Settle myself down on these feed sacks. Hey kids! Huh.
Too shy to even stare like regular kids. Well, won't bother
ya. I'll just get comfortable here. Don't mind me.

HABITS: heavy smoker, Export A unfiltered, heavy beer
drinker, some rye and ginger. Loaned a lot of money to
buddies. Eddy Penner admits to $200. (Check this one. Has a
record from Alberta.) Dean Wall borrowed $400. Gambler.
John Mason borrowed $300. Drunk driving charges on this
one. There's more owed than this. See the initials and dollar
amounts found in back of subject's phone book. Get more
information on these. Possible motive here.

Of all the Jeezelly luck! These farmers musta taken some
long way around town and headed back home again. I
nodded off and missed it, way to hellangone in the bloody
sticks I am! Those dumb asses were too bunged-up
to even stop and tap me on the shoulder and wake me up,
for chrissakes! Least they coulda done, they give me a lift,
they coulda got rid of me just as easy.

No sign of 'em. Let's see here. Long driveway all mudded
up. Guess it's easier for 'em to leave the truck out here.
Well, I'm not going to bother that bunch. I'll stick my
thumb out again.

What's this then? New blacktop? God Almighty, where is this hick heaven? Looks halfways like the old Maxwell ranch, same hills, but this isn't the road, no way. That there's a river big enough to be the Peace. We must be near Taylor Flats but I don't see the refinery, don't smell it either. Huh. Still, except there's too much land brushed off, this looks like Maxwell's place. I could swear...so Mum and Pop's would be just half a mile down there but hell, what am I thinking? Better keep walking down this brand new road. Somebody'll be along soon, good road like this.

Last contact with family on June 28. Had supper with them. Bought expensive cowboy boots. Went out with Eddy Penner that evening to cabarets in Fort St. John. Drove back to the Hudson's Hope trailer park early in the morning. Estimate between 2:30 and 3:30 a.m. on June 29. Penner too drunk to remember any of it. Claims to have woken up on his own couch around noon on the 29th. No girlfriends in the picture, according to Penner, Wall and Mason. Parents never met any girlfriends either.

This is nuts! If that place isn't ours, I'll eat my shirt. What's this say, then?

"PROPERTY OF B.C. HYDRO.
SITE E FLOOD ZONE.
TRESPASSERS WILL BE PROSECUTED.
APRIL, 1992."

Dream on! I oughta know! No way it's this far downstream, no way, not with us almost done the Bennett Dam. Plus that 1992 business is a laugh. Spelling mistake off 20 plus years. Hopeless! And somebody got paid to print that sign up and nail it to this old gate of ours.

REUBEN

By God, it *is* our gate! Wire's off of it, still, I helped Pop build that heavy old thing! Now look at this! No corrals. No barn. No pig houses, chicken house, nothing! No house. But that's how Mum had the garden, I swear. I'll just walk up there to the hill.

Hole for the cellar. Somebody's torched it all. Holy crow.

My God! That's a regular lake down where the river is. Was. I'm all back-asswards here, this gives me the willies. I better hike down to that Mennonite place and get my bearings straight. If I give 'em gas money, they might just drive me to town.

EDUCATION: dropped out in Grade 8. Occupation: heavy equipment operator. Latest work place: W.A.C. Bennett Dam, north of Hudson's Hope, B.C. Has also worked as roughneck on gas rigs in Fort Nelson area from 1964-66. Reliable work record at Dam site according to foreman, Jake Hills. Took two weeks off in May, 1968, to help father put crop in. Parent's farm in Cecil Lake.

Yo! Hey! It's the same truck, those farmers! Stop! Silly old fart drives twenty-five miles an hour and takes a hundred yards to stop. Jeez! Try and run in these damn new boots, kills my feet. Wait! Look at him picking something up off the road, old scavenger. Looks like a crowbar. Hey, I'll just hop in back if you're headed to town, are ya? Guess that's a nod, what an oaf! I'm gonna ask Pop about this bunch.

CAROLINE WOODWARD

Well, this is a lucky break. Hoo boy, get my wind back. Let's look this over now. Same hills, I'll swear, except for this lake. Now, this is some new kind of bridge coming up. My God! They backed up the Beatton on us, crazy, I'm going crazy! Hey! Do I hafta bash your window in? Stop!

Bank account not touched since reported missing, July 1, 1968. Put account on active file for five years. Maintain on inactive for five more years until July 1, 1979. No activity whatsoever.

Waste of breath! Old fart's deaf as well as stunned. May as well take it easy and try and pry it outa him when we get to town. Look, there's the cut-off to the old bridge. I've got all my marbles, no mistake. I'll wait on this, no panic. Nope.

Sure is a short-cut we're taking. I can see the elevators already. What's this? He's slowing down for this bunch of cars. We're a ways outa town, what's up now? No use trying to get his attention now, look's like he's pulling in here. Elks Hall.

Brand new Elks Hall, looks like. Or else just new siding. Moved out here to the boonies. I better just hop off here and get on downtown. Ackland's be closed by the time I get there at this rate. Well! That's Mrs. Gerhardt and her old aunt! Better wave at 'em or Mother will never hear the end of it. That's the McManus tribe. Old man looks like hell. Should poke my nose in and see what's up. Half the country's here.

REUBEN

Packed house. All the old geezers in their suits. Now what's he on about? Oh boy, it's a preacher! Better take my cap off. Oughta slip out. None of my business anyway. Oh Jeez, that young fella's turned around and seen me, staring right at me, it's...!

You're here! It's you! Reuben, come back here! It's me, Stevie! Steve! Don't look away from me, damn you, Reub! You should of come back before this! Pop's gone! He hung on, hoping for you, Reuben. He never believed it. Reuben!

No. No, no, no. This isn't right. I'm not supposed to be here, no, Stevie, stay put. I'm going. I know. I'm gone. It's okay. I'll find him. Be good. I'm gone now.

Reuben Adam Fehr. Inactive file. Leads exhausted. Foul play suspected. Unsubstantiated. Case closed.

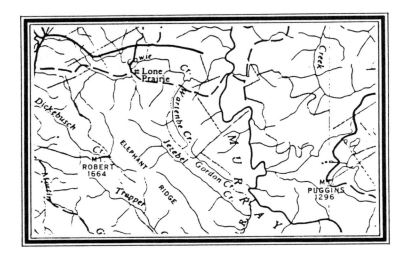

Good Dog

She is out on the land, walking with the dog for company in case the long shadows by the spruce bluffs turn into bears. For years, the neighbour's old work horses have been led to the middle of the bluffs, then shot by her husband with his Army rifle, a .303.

She gets the shivers by that place and usually takes the long way to avoid it. Sometimes she is daydreaming so much that she forgets and comes to, with a tingling jolt, stops dead, in the purple shade of the bluff with the trees all creaking and soft horse talk right behind her. Then she runs as hard and fast as she can, not stopping once down the big hill to the next open field.

The dog is good company for the shivers and the heart-thumping run after. He races alongside her, grinning, nipping at her calves until she smacks him. He can't help it, his instincts are to herd everything that moves, the faster the better.

Today she is taking the long way down to the river breaks, checking on the Big Slough to see if it's dried up completely. She calls the dog to heel. This is another test.

Sometimes the rustling of dry cutthroat grass in the slough is more than a travelling family of fieldmice. Once it was the neighbour's sullen young bull, the Red Angus with the long Scottish name. The dog went straight for it, whether he was playing the Decoy/Hero for her sake or just practising his herding instincts, she wasn't sure. She walked backwards, slowly, calmly, for nearly two hundred yards and crawled under the barb-wire fence.

The Big Slough has a thick, green crust of water left in it, not even enough for ducks. Dog runs in short, leaping bursts through the high hay grass, timothy and brome, hoping for a flurry of prairie chicken wings, anything but the high-pitched racket of squirrels which is all he gets today.

Dog is not yet three, unmated, a Collie-Shepherd cross with something farther back that gives him yellow eyes.

He doubles back to the walking Woman, checking in, she's fine, his ears straining, all eyes on the wide, white face. She has spoken, the quiet Flemish words along with this lovely ear scratch she does almost absent-mindedly. He only understands one word. Yes. And he leaps away, legs like pistons, ecstasy in every cell, racing beside the ten acre strip of ripe barley like a coiled-up wild thing finally sprung free.

Yes. Run along. I'm safe. Good dog, run along. Yes, you heard me!

The wagon trail is hard-packed, rutted in a few low spots where the run-off water settled and spring machinery gouged into the mud. He knows better than to run in the barley, knocking the dry, ripe heads off, getting the sharp spears between his toes, in his ears, or worse, poking at his eyes.

His nose trolls the lowest band of air, passing up stale mouse trails. He moves up a notch, still running easily, catching two faint whiffs of deadmeat somewhere. What's this then? Somewhere to the south.

Bird it is, some whiskey jack broke his neck against a poplar tree. Freak accident. That's Mother Nature for you.

As far as Dog is concerned, whiskey jacks are in the same league as squirrels and they stay through the winters. They come closer and closer to the House, waiting for the human slop bucket to be emptied or picking through cowshit for undigested grains, shrieking if he so much as looked at them sideways. Disgusting, noisy things with no fear to speak of. Lucky for them they fly. Same goes for magpies and crows. Flashy rodents with wings is all they are.

Dog's nose is out of joint by now with these home movies flickering in his skull. Dog dislikes ridicule. He has a job to do, daily routines to maintain, training to continue. If only they would let him herd the beasts!

Wait! Bloodflesh! A big thing, no mistake, where now, where? Aha, oh yes! Downwind from the breaks. Below the saskatoons, almost ripe. Through the fence, quick

now, oh boy, stop. Stop you fool! It's a big one, get away!
A mother one, a mad cow mother. Oh boyoboy.

Dog boots it back under the fence and the cow, still
bawling, throat hoarse, keeps running beside it. Up and
down, up and down. My baby, my baby! I'll kill you, horn
your guts, crush your black fur face! My baby, my mur-
dered baby boy! She wails. She keens in cow rage, cow
grief. Dog knows it. Stays well back on his side of the
fence. End of play time, run-along-free-adventure-time
for Dog.

The Woman hears the cow long before she sees her
running along the fence dividing the leased range land
from the field of alfalfa. No living thing could mistake
that animal's anguish. That is the only word for it. Anguish.
The big Hereford is wild with grief and pain. Her udder is
swollen with at least two days of unused milk. She is a
range beef cow, never milked by hand, six years old. This
is not the time to try.

Dog leads the way on the safe side of the fence and they
both stop when the crows fly up in a black clump. A small
Hereford leg lies gleaming on a hillside. The crows return
to a spot just beyond the hill, near a stand of young poplars.
The Woman has seen enough to know it's a bear most
likely. Poor momma cow.

Momma Cow will join the others down by the river
when she gets over it. She will babysit the other calves.
She will kill the first bloody bear who shows his stinking,
meat-eating face near those calves the way that empty-
headed Shorthorn heifer should have done yesterday.
One last dry sob and sigh.

Dog and the Woman turn away from the river and head
back inland. Cow has subsided and stands with her broad

brown back to them, facing the river, feeling a tremendous thirst coming on.

The Woman deliberately walks past the bluffs for the first time in six years, taking the short-cut home, covering her ears with her hands to drown out the rustling, murmuring sounds. Dog sticks close to her. All stations alert. One lungful of musky bear is enough to give anyone the shakes. He has a job to do. Escort service, bodyguard, plainclothes man, call it what you will. Dog dares you to try anything funny. Dog leaves a trail of piss laden with fear and loathing all the way from the breaks to the House.

□   □   □

All night Dog dreams of herding little white-faced calves and their large, brown mothers across fields of sweet-smelling alfalfa to a scoop-out full of cold, good-smelling water. Then he herds them to another field of high yellow and white clover where they eat some more. He understands them perfectly.

They say, "Thank you! You're such a good Dog!" and he says, "Just doing my job the best I know how, Ladies. Some alsike clover thataway, a little variety perhaps?" And they understand him perfectly and say in their deep, sexy cow voices, "Thanks so much! We really appreciate it, you know how it is with new calves again and all that." Dog cocks his head sideways in a disarming little gesture and restrains himself from squirming with the pleasure of it all. Finally, he herds them, ever so skillfully and with no muss, fuss or panic to the spruce bluffs where they all lay down in the cool shade and chew their cuds, burping their cow burps in the efficient double-stomached way they have, while the calves nap after their midday milk break.

The old work horses get up from their piles of tired bones and rub against the trunks of trees to relieve their itchy spots and harness-pressure points. They visit with each other, standing side by side with old colleagues, swapping stories about threshing gangs way back when, the glory days, heroic mid-winter trips to the Red Cross Outpost Hospital in the middle of the night, and so forth. They go back a long way, at least twenty to thirty years each, but they never get much past the primes of their lives when they swap stories, which is a blessing, isn't it, for they had been well cared for and feared nothing after the terrible shock of gelding. Not even the last shambling walk, the last feed of oats from the can the men brought with them into this cool, quiet tree-place. The deer flies and noseeumms never bother them in here and everything tastes and smells like the best chopped grain, spring grass, and the water like chilled alfalfa tea. It's a wonderful thing.

Dog leaves all of them there. He'll be back tomorrow, all is well. And he dreams of morning. How he supervises the chores, the opening of the chicken-house door, the collection of eggs, the opening of the pig-house doors, the pouring of chop and water into the troughs. Then the walk up the hill to the barn. Opening the top half of the Dutch doors to the streaming light dancing with dust motes, waiting for the Man to finish milking the Holstein, to trot alongside him when they return to the House. Mission accomplished.

There will be a pan of boiled wheat, fresh water, some cold, cooked food, a moose bone perhaps. She will say in English, "Good morning, Doggie!" Reward for a job well done. Patrol completed safely. All is well. Good Dog.

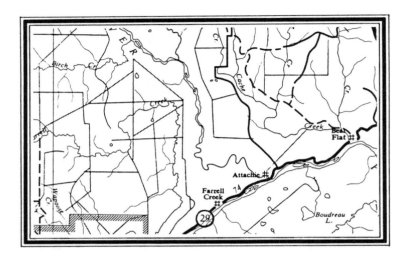

I Dream of Looking Skyward, Praying for Rain, with Water up to my Knees and Rising

The herd of several hundred cattle moves slowly up the valley. Three riders wearing handkerchiefs over their noses and mouths follow, one on right and one on left flank, one roving near the tail end.

A woman's voice comes through to the rider's beeper on right flank. "We gotta start pushing them, Carl! It's five o'clock already and it's only half a mile from you!"

"Okay, Shirl, pass it on to Jake, willya? I got my hands full here."

I STAND LOOKING SKYWARD

The pace quickens, the dust thickens, and the theme from Bonanza is amplified from Shirl's truck on the hill overlooking the herd. Behind the truck are large red barns, corrals, four long, white sheds, and a two-storey farm house painted buttercup yellow. In one of the corrals, six youngsters are leading two-year-old Aberdeen Angus steers around in a circle. Three judges, two men and a woman with clipboards, watch and scribble and tick off points.

Inside one long, white shed are hutches filled with chickens of all shapes, colours and sizes. There are also rabbits huddled inside their hutches next to the chickens and a row of cats, some with kittens. On the wall across from the small animals and fowl are sheaves of wheat, oats, barley, and crested rye. On the tables are jars of alfalfa and clover seed and a row of honey jars, through which a shaft of light is glowing so that the shades of honey from palest fireweed to amber buckwheat gleam like liquid jewels in jars.

Next to this shed, in a huge red barn, are pens filled with pigs — pink, white, black, spotted and striped. Except for the lively teenage wiener pigs, the others are comatose in the straw. One massive sow has twelve piglets nursing as she sprawls on her side, a gracious mixture of competence and nonchalance. The stalls opposite the porkers are occupied by cattle, standing or lying on sweet-smelling oat straw. Industrious youngsters are washing down Holstein calves with buckets of water and brushes. One little girl is using a hairbrush on her calf's broad black and white forehead, making little curls in pleasing designs.

"Daisy Mae West Wind Grandmere, you are the best in the West no matter what anyone else says," she murmurs.

planting a kiss on the pink eraser nose. ''And you're a girl so you won't get sold and killed by Overwaitea, either.'' Outside in the ring, the Aberdeen Angus steers are lined up in show stance with the judges, in immaculate whites, walking up to each youngster, saying a few words, then fastening blue, red, white or yellow rosettes on the show halters. Once more, they promenade around the ring with parents beaming from the rails. The twelve-year-olds attempt to keep serious expressions on their faces except for one freckled little redhead whose steer has a second-place red rosette on his brand new halter.

''Ma,'' he hisses in a stage whisper. ''Ma, Charlie is bein' so good! Didja see 'im when that big one bolted?!''

The tall red-haired woman with four more freckled, red-haired kids clinging to the rails waves at him, putting a finger to her lips, nodding, smiling, blowing her nose, and nodding some more.

As this group leaves, the next group of youngsters, most of whom are about four feet tall, bring in their calves. Two calves bolt immediately upon entering the corral, dragging their humans behind them. The others clump up at one end of the ring, suddenly uncertain of showing procedures. Several tykes take the precaution of digging in their heels in wide-legged stances, grimly anchoring their lead ropes around their waists.

''Manage your animals!'' calls out the senior judge. All three judges contrive to put on glum faces as they survey the pint-sized calf-tamers. Several boys wear little string ties and white cowboy hats, and all of them are wearing stiff new blue jeans and white shirts.

Eventually, a little procession commences in a clockwise direction and with discreet assistance from the judges, an orderly line-up is formed in the centre of the ring. All six calves receive ribbons as there were ties for second and third place. A proud parade around the ring begins. One of the judges advises the crowd of onlookers to hold their applause until the competitors have left the ring, wisely preventing a mini-stampede.

"Last beef entry of the day in the 4-H Division, ladies and gentlemen, boys and girls. Pardon me, that's a dairy class, we've just had the last beef class, a fine group of young-sters in their first year showing spring calves very well indeed. A promising group of young competitors. Now we'll have a look at the senior dairy project. Ring One. Senior Dairy." The announcer's voice booms through his megaphone.

Five teenagers leading Holstein heifers walk around in a stately circle. They wear spotless white shirts and slacks and carry short, white canes. One heifer calmly dumps liquid green manure behind her as she follows her master. Her gleaming flanks and shampooed heels stain alfalfa green. The competitor behind her smirks, unaware that his own Buttercup Empress Conacher is inspired to launch an even larger load of cowflops over *her* carefully groomed backside. A contagious giggle ripples around the corral rails, while the oblivious show participants march stiffly alongside the ambling heifers.

Inside the large yellow farmhouse, Muriel Brown and Dai Thomas are judging vegetables. It's a very large ex-hibit and it's hot. They've been at it since 8 a.m. that morning.

"Let's finish up this lot and have an orange-ade break," wheezes Dai.

"I couldn't agree more," responds Muriel gratefully. Dai

CAROLINE WOODWARD

Thomas is the Senior Judge, and she is his assistant for the first time this year. It's quite an honour for her, in her opinion.

"Peas! Bloody peas! Carrots, spuds, beets, and turnips I can single out in a minute. But peas!" he fumes, tapping his clipboard none too gently with his pencil.

"Let's see," she says, briskly. "Uniform size, not over-blown, no scars, open up a pod for size. Proper showing." Her hands shell one pea pod per plate as she lists the judging criteria.

"Look here! Under-size, over-size, white fungus! Here we go, three decent specimens. Let's count peas to the pod. Seven, six, eight! Taste finally...all good, let's give it to our top producer here. Hah! Four minutes flat. Ribbons please, sir!"

"Good work, lass. Now let's slip over to the concession stand and get something to sustain us through the ruddy useless marrows and pumpkins, shall we?"

Despite the 30° C. heat, Dai Thomas wears a tweed suit coat and matching vest and pants. At the start of the day he wore a brown pork-pie hat on his mop of grey hair. He abandoned it mid-way through the red and green cabbages.

"And how are you making out, Mr. Thomas, Miss Brown?" asks the little woman in the Women's Institute concession booth as she hands them their drinks.

"Good showing, despite the drought," says Dai, after a healthy swig. "Would you mind topping that up for me? Thirsty work, this."

"Oh certainly, Mr. Thomas," she flutters. Her daughter's coddled vegetable marrow is on show in all its pale-skinned glory, started in February with a special light-bulb in the house, of all things!

"Thank you kindly, Mrs. Morrow," says Dai, reaching up for his hat brim to tug, but ending up making a little salute instead. They return to the Vegetable Shed, refreshed and ready to do battle with the finer points of vegetable showmanship: true-to-type, ripeness, absence of mechanical, bacterial, or viral damage, and the interior evidence of regular watering, hilling and soil preparation.

"You'll be pleased to see there are only four marrows on exhibit," says Muriel. "Two unfit for showing, what a waste to pick them so small! This thing is huge, and this one is fair-to-middling. What to do?"

"The ribbons, Madam. Although we might want to withhold a first place in this sorry lot. Bloody shame they were invented in the first place. Who eats them, I ask you?"

"Some people stuff them with bread and raisins."

"Agghh! Bloody horrible!"

They proceed to the major garden exhibits that take pride of place on the long paper-covered table. Some are artfully arranged in wicker baskets, cornucopia style. Some are placed on massive cardboard podiums, sheathed in green crepe paper. Still others are displayed in camouflaged baby chick boxes, the kind they arrive in off the plane from Edmonton hatcheries. Eight garden vegetables and two varieties of annual garden flowers. Snapdragons, clarkia, bachelor buttons and cosmos are the hardy favourites, while sweetpeas fill the air with their heady fragrance. Homemade labels indicating variety (Nantes Half-long Carrots), (Homesteader Peas), (Detroit Dark Red Beets), (Ultra Girl Tomatoes) are strategically placed in each exhibit.

Dai has his doubts about the most magnificent display. It's due to the tomatoes.

CAROLINE WOODWARD

"It doesn't say they're greenhouse-raised, but I'll bet my bottom dollar they are — and the label ought to say so," he pronounces, after a lengthy deliberation. "We *are* looking at Best of Show category, after all."

Muriel studies the problematic tomatoes. "To tell the truth, I much prefer this display here," she says, pointing to a converted baby-chick box lined with oat straw. "Three varieties of potato, two each of carrot, turnip, beet and late lettuce. Beautiful stuff. Lovely old-fashioned flower bouquet, perfect pickling cukes, and three types of bean, all in prime condition. It's more representative of a family garden than this flashy effort." She points to the huge tomatoes nestled beside English cucumbers and green peppers.

"I'm torn, I truly am," he declares. "We can't fault any-one for going all-out with a greenhouse and forcing stuff along. It's no easy feat to beat the frost in this country with the likes of these." They contemplate the hothouse beauties glumly. "We have, here," he stands up straight, "a dilemma on our hands. To reward new advances and vigilance in northern horticulture, or the steadfast virtues of a bountiful family garden, the tried and true."

She looks for a technicality to break the tie. A missing label, too few or too many vegetables per plate, a concealed sunburn, perhaps a clever fingernail nicking off potato scab. Sighing, she hefts a tomato from each exhibit and looks at her confounded colleague.

"The knife, sir."

The evidence is plain to both sets of eyes. Dai hands Muriel a magnificent blue rosette to arrange on the display with firm, red vine-ripened tomatoes while the watery discharge from the hothouse experiment leaks onto the green crepe paper bedding of the more elaborate exhibit. "A job well done," he says, saluting her. "Decisiveness, experience and a solid command of show vegetable criteria, these things the astute judge must possess," he says, tapping his clipboard for emphasis and smiling. "Furthermore, anyone who grows three varieties of potato commands more respect than a green pepper dilettante, in my books, speaking quite confidentially to a fellow judge," he adds, offering his arm as they stroll down the aisles of prize-winning produce to retrieve the pork-pie hat back in red cabbages.

It must be said that in the lemon meringue pie section of Shed Three, these diplomatic qualities are abandoned as two formidable judges argue their respective positions. Should spectacular height and emerging weepiness of meringue win out over a pie of superior lemon taste but a slightly tough and dense topping of meringue? Mrs. Gough and Mrs. Large are battling over fourth place, and since each thinks the other is actually the assistant, a major war of wills is underway.

Elsewhere in Shed Three, judges are pleased to report a trebling of entries in the whole-wheat and health-type bread selections. The Parker House rolls are as difficult as ever to place in a hierarchy. 'Such uniform excellence is a pleasure to contend with!' they state in their notes.

The mitred corners of place-mats, seam finishes on cotton housedresses, and the backing of quilts are closely inspected by a bevy of needlework experts. The 4-H record books containing samples of interfacing, buttonholes and plackets are set open at especially outstanding pages by the District Home Economist. She is surrounded by hundreds of hours of hand sewing and machine stitching by girls of ten and young women of seventeen. And, she acknowledges with a wry grimace, by mothers who despaired of nagging errant young homebodies-in-training to finish in time for the Fair.

"She'd rather do it herself 'cuz she's a picky little thing, and I don't have the patience on the machine," says one mother to another as they carry their lawn chairs over to where the 4-H modelling will begin.

"You don't say ," responds Mom No. 2. "Well, my Melissa won't let me set a hand near her work, ever! Won't let me help her pick out colours or anything. Just wait till you see her model this wild housecoat today! The leader hates it, tried to talk her out of it."

"Your Missy," says Mom No. 1, "is gonna end up a fashion designer, and all because of 4-H. Brenda would rather order from Sears to tell you the truth, so she can look like town kids. Doesn't care how much money she saves if she sews. But I just say right back, when you got your own money you can buy what you like, Lady Di!"

Mom No. 2 beams and scowls unconvincingly and beams again. "Don't know who she takes after, our Missy." She smoothes her own navy and white striped polyster pant suit with sweating palms. "She's top of the class in her high school home-ec class, but she's a bit too snazzy for 4-H. Everybody else's housecoats are corduroy and velveteen, but Melissa's got fake tiger fur with slippers to match! They gotta give it to her for making her own accessories, don't you think? They're not store-bought."

"Oh, sure, I wouldn't be surprised," obliges Mom No. 1 who is silently counting her blessings that her Brenda chose sky-blue, fine-waled corduroy for her housecoat project and not some wacky fur stuff like you-know-who's kid did.

I STAND LOOKING SKYWARD

A crowd of more than one hundred sweating people sit on the bleachers waiting for the horse show. In the first ring, five quarter horses are led in and promenade in a circle. Three old gents hanging on the rails pick out the equine winners and speculate what the judge, a tall, angular man in a ten-gallon hat, might say about the conformation of the horsewomen.

"An easy-keeper, that one," says one old geezer from the side of his mouth, nodding at a hefty woman in skin-tight pea-green jeans and a filled-to-bursting frilly pink cowgirl shirt.

"Highstrung type over there," says another. A bony woman in English riding habit stalks beside a skittish bay, hissing at it constantly. "Walk! Walk! Walk!" The bay's eyes roll back, flashing white.

The group is called to a halt. A sorrel mare steps out smartly, extending front and back legs, flaring her silvery tail and raising her head, eyes bright and ears perked forward. A small, silver-haired woman with a tanned, unlined face holds the lead rope of the sorrel and speaks softly to it.

"That one's worth a mint," says one of the gents on the rails. "Little Missus Greeley there, she trains and boards some very expensive stock on her place."

"Looks to have some A-rab. Lookit that little dish face on it, pretty thing," comments another. "Might not have quite enough hindquarters for a true-to-type quarter horse though. Don't know how the judge'll see it."

"Tell ya, it's already won the gait class with Missus Greeley for senior women *and* junior boys with her young nephew on it, did real well, so it's the same judge for gait as conformation," noted the first gent, a secret admirer of anything Missus Greeley is connected with.

Three of the horses jump at a horn blaring, bumping into each other like a domino effect. The sorrel stays calm and steps away from the irritable threesome. The dark chestnut led by the heavy-set woman in pink and green has its ears laid back, tossing its head in a bad-tempered manner.

"Madam, keep your horse to one side, please," calls the judge.

The woman starts to sputter a protest, but the judge walks over to inspect the leg of the high-strung bay beside it.

"Walk your horse, please."

The tall, thin woman walks the bay forward and brings it back in a small circle. Her horse is definitely favouring one back leg. The judge nods and frowns. He pulls out his clipboard, makes notes, and pulls the ribbons from his shirt pocket.

The metallic rumble of approaching helicopters coincides with strange sounds from the main Fair loudspeaker, but the jeeps are among them first. Then the sky above the Fairgrounds is filled with helicopters in formation. One boy counts thirty as he hides in the horse barn.

Muriel Brown and Dai Thomas come out from under the awning of the Women's Institute Tent. "What in blazes do we have here then?" Dai demands to know, dabbing at mustard on his chin.

"Good heavens, I don't have a clue! Do you recognize that fellow with the loudspeaker?" Muriel points at a tall man with a hawkish profile bellowing into the loudspeaker. She grips her paper plate, with raspberry shortcake on it, with both hands and stares at the speaker, who seems vaguely familiar.

The rumble of the helicopters drowns out his words. He looks up angrily and reaches for a beeper into which he shouts. The helicopters move up and sideways like a huge cloud of silver and black grasshoppers. People stare after them, while the cattle bawl in the barns, several horses rear in the ring, and chickens squawk in confusion.

"Read my lips!" Hawknose yells, looking at his right-hand man with a smirk. Righthand smirks back.

"Everyone, attention!" Hawknose bellows. Then there is silence except for several babies and the sounds of the animals. "This is an emergency evacuation. You are asked at this time to leave the Fairgrounds by the west gate, on foot. Do not worry about the livestock at this time. I repeat, leave by the west gate. Begin immediately."

Absolute silence for a split-second. The phalanx of helicopters drones unheeded. Then the roar of hundreds of voices. The crowd surges forward in a great, ragged wave. Men and women yell the names of each other, their children, their aged parents. The children are big-eyed and silent until their arms are tugged by grown-ups. Muriel cannot believe her eyes. The 4-H pledge comes unbidden to her mind. *I pledge my head to clearer thinking.* She tries to think.

Telescopic rifles are raised by the men in jeeps. She counts over twenty grey jeeps before she loses track.

"Let's skedaddle, Eldon," hisses a young woman near Muriel. She pulls a toddler back from the main body of the crowd and keeps one arm curved around a very new baby. The noise is deafening as the jeeps rev up and the helicopters advance slowly. Shots are fired over the crowd as the jeepmen begin to herd them toward the west gate. A child runs by, almost bumping into Dai Thomas, carrying a large black rabbit which stares pinkly at the world. An elderly woman clutches a jar of peaches and her handbag.

CAROLINE WOODWARD

"Turn the animals loose!" yells a teenage girl as she dodges a jeep and runs toward the barns. Two others join her, one boy in an all-white dairy show outfit and a young woman in a semi-formal velvet dress with silver sandals. Her tiara falls off, and she kicks her sandals from her feet to sprint through the crowd.

Muriel turns to speak to Dai but he isn't beside her. She ducks back into the Supper Tent and crawls out under the opposite side. She stays low as she runs behind the outdoor toilets and heads for the parking lot.

Too late. Five jeeps guard it and the men have rifles ready. Several people are turned back to join the crowd on foot. The jeep closest to her has a wolf tail dangling from the antennae. Phone! She has to get to a phone. There must be one in the old yellow house.

Except for a small stampede of calves and sheep, almost all the people are beyond the main thoroughfare of the grounds. The helicopters hover over them. She decides to make a dash through the cattle that are being chased out of the barn, but a jeep swerves around the corner. Five men wearing rubber pig masks and holding cellular phones sit in it, pointing at her. The driver leans on the horn continually, but two monstrous bulls, one Charolais, one Red Polled Shorthorn, amble in front of the vehicle. Muriel uses the moment to dash into the yellow house.

A pot of tea and several cups, steam still rising from them, are abandoned at the old formica table. The house is still and quiet except for a radio somewhere upstairs. An old-fashioned black telephone on the wall next to her is dead. She slams her hand on the door jamb. The faded yellow gingham curtains flutter and another jeep roars past. She ducks and then, staying low, she finds the stairs and makes her way up.

"...the farmer needs the rain, and the farmer needs the heat, needs it in the proper order, just to grow a field of wheat..." The radio plays on, and Muriel slips over to the window in an upstairs bedroom. She sees Mrs. Greeley jump the sorrel mare, riding bareback, over the low fence behind the concession stands. She sees a small red-haired boy yanking at the lead rope of his steer. "C'mon, Charlie, c'mon!" he begs, near tears.

"...But when the wind keeps a blowin', blowin' everything away, you can bet your boots the farmer's gonna pay..." Muriel backs away from the window and looks for another phone. A modern push-button unit beside the radio is dead. Then she hears a different kind of motor noise, a higher pitch than the jeeps. Right past the porch downstairs roars Dai Thomas with an elderly woman in a print housedress on the back of a motorcycle. Horrified, Muriel watches as a jeep turns to follow them, two jeepmen standing up, aiming their rifles. She races down the stairs and through the kitchen.

"NO!" she screams, jumping off the steps of the kitchen door, landing in front of the jeep. It swerves in a spray of gravel and dust.

"Get a move on, lady," one jeepman snaps, waving the rifle at her. She turns and runs.

She can hear the jeep stall and a curse, as she zig-zags into the first red barn. I am in a violent American movie, she thinks. I am even running away from men with rifles. I am in shock. *My heart to greater loyalty.*

A dappled grey horse stands with her lead rope untied, one end on the ground in front of her. The jeep roars past the barn. She walks slowly toward the mare, murmuring,

"Don't bolt, lovey, don't bolt." The mare cocks her head but stays put until she follows Muriel to a wooden pen.

She climbs up the slats of the pen, trying to ignore the huge sow sniffing at her legs and the piglets squealing in the straw. She turns awkwardly, urging the horse closer until she can get one leg slung over its back. With a push and leap, she straddles the horse and walks her over to the open doors. She can see one jeep circling at the eastern end of the grounds and several men walking into the Vegetable Shed.

She leans over the mare's neck to tie the lead rope in a single loop, trusting the horse to neck-rein. Then she takes a deep breath and digs in her heels. The mare trots and then, with another dig and a slap on the rump, she breaks into a lope as they head out the door.

"Oh, you sweetheart!" whispers Muriel as the mare turns left again without breaking stride in an easy rocking-chair gait. She hears a shout behind her and sees, straight ahead, a closed barbed-wire gate.

"Omigod! No!" She hauls back on the rope, hearing another shout and the roar of a jeep. The mare plunges forward and Muriel grabs for the coarse black mane, thinking, crazily, of a teenage Elizabeth Taylor in *National Velvet*. Without so much as a lurch, they soar over the gate and gallop down the road.

In seconds they reach another gate but this one is already open, lying in a tangled mess of wire and poles on the ground. Muriel manages to slow the mare to a walk, patting her neck as she neatly picks up her feet and negotiates the fallen gate.

She pushes her to a lope again as they come to a large hay field with alfalfa lying in swaths and equipment standing idle at one end. She stops and listens, looking skyward. Helicopters travel in a long line more than a mile away from where she is. She turns the horse to follow the edge of the field, staying close to the fringe of trees so she can head under cover at the first sound of motors coming closer. When she reaches the end of the field, she decides to go through a thinly wooded stretch of poplars.

In minutes they emerge onto high banks with sage and saskatoon bushes everywhere. There is no fence so she risks being out in the open to move forward to a look-out point.

"I've got to see where they're going," she says aloud. The mare perks up her ears.

She rides toward a smallish clump of chokecherries and young poplars, high enough to camouflage both horse and rider. She is close enough to see the long line of people and aghast to see a dirty brown tide of water lapping only ten feet from the top of the bank. A big herd of cattle is climbing up the opposite side of the valley, water at their heels. She thinks she hears the Bonanza theme song from very far away.

She squints and strains to see better, but the Fairground people are tiny figures. She recognizes animals by their shapes and she sees the jeeps. Then she hears the gun-shots. The tiny people are walking into the water, and the shots keep ringing out, even as the heads bob and the arms thrash in the water. She sees a large white cow drop and roll end-over-end down the ridge and into the water. The helicopters swerve overhead.

"The bastards! They're shooting from overhead!" she shrieks. The mare jumps a little but calms down as she pats her shoulder and neck. She tries to calm herself down as well, but this is impossible. She cannot stand to look at the ridge again or to keep listening to the piercing screams. Human or animal? She can't tell anymore.

She looks down and sees the water spilling over the bank nearest to her.

"We've got to head for the highway, little girl," she says to the mare, crossing the field in the open. This time they jump both gates, Muriel nearly losing her seat at the tangled gate as the mare swerves a little to clear the mess safely. She congratulates herself for wearing her culotte skirt and sensible walking shoes for her day of judging. She stifles a nervous laugh which threatens to go on and on. *My hands to larger service.*

They gallop straight through the deserted Fairgrounds and race for the entrance to the highway. They run alongside the old asphalt road on the dirt shoulder and come to the first intersection. She slows the mare down to look at the signpost.

It is a gleaming blue and yellow sign, shaped like an unfurling flag. The dirt is freshly dug around the base of the post. An old black and white sign lays in the ditch. She doesn't want to dismount because she has never been very good about mounting bareback like a Cossack. She needs a perch, a boost, or some artificial aid, but once she's onboard, she stays on. She feels nausea rising and the shakes getting to her hands and knees. The new sign says New Horizon, Unincorporated. *That's nonsense!*

The old sign in the ditch says what it said this morning when she drove past it at 7:30 a.m. Peace Country Fairgrounds, 1 km.

She clucks to the horse and they move forward, staying off the asphalt. With luck, they could reach town in three hours. *Someone would tell them what happened. It would be on the news.* She could stop at the first farm house and use the phone, but she doesn't count on it working. She leans down and pats the sweaty grey neck again. *The Department of Agriculture is going to hear about this on the news!* And where were the trusty R.C.M.P.? Had no one gotten to a phone? Muriel chants the 4-H pledge to keep her wits about her.

...And my health to better living,
for my club, my community, and my country.

The wind picks up, blowing a fine dust of topsoil in her face. She bows her head against the grit. The drought is going on twenty-five days, she thinks. It'll ruin us all. She fights back a shudder. Nothing is right anymore. Everyone's gone and the air smells like water.

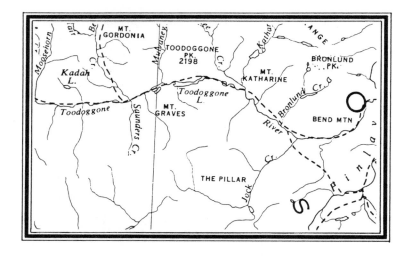

Finding Due North

I may as well pretend to sleep back here. Good God, my head hurts. Serves me right for partying all night like a silly fool. Ugh. That dog reeks. Peeyuu. I hope to God I don't get sick if I close my eyes. Good thing I threw up back in Cache Creek, got rid of the worst of it, I think. Oh God, nine more hours with this craftsperson, artist-woman, whatever, and that slobbering hound and my head pounding like crazy. Puhleeze, kick in extra-strength pills, c'mon! I can't believe I'm in this awful hippy bus! Look at it, feathers, Haida buttons, Stein buttons, sagebrush hanging everywhere! She's barely emerged from the sixties by the looks of it. I can't handle middle-aged earth mothers. Lord. I can't imagine what her so-called art is like. Ugh. Why the Foundation lumped us all together like this is beyond me. Ahh, thank God for codeine. Oooo. They could have done a nice little televised event in Vancouver, where we could've gotten our awards, hobnobbed with the magazine and publishing and gallery people, smiled, shook hands, thank you ever so much, bang, all done. But oh no, they've got to send us up to some godforsaken college for a week-end seminar or some such claptrap. Extract a few panel discussions out of us, give the locals a primer in aesthetics.

Owww, she drives too fast on these rotten curves! Still, if MAN-MADE EARTHWORKS sells in the States, I can't complain. Must rattle Liang's chains on that score when I get back to civilization. There's bound to be somebody of import at this conference, symposium, whatever. "Finding Due North: The Multi-Media Approach." Not a great title. Not bad though.

THE DRIVER'S SEAT
One Irate Silk Quilt Artist

He doesn't want to talk to me. He hates my dog. So he's got a bad hangover. Great. Let him stew in it! I don't care how great a photographer he is, he's a grouch and a snob and a total loss as far as company is concerned. Afraid of the mountains. Huh. Can't drive till we get to Williams Lake. Fine. I'll drive the Pine Pass and when he wants to go to Tumbler Ridge again, we won't, because I don't. All those aerial shots must have cost a mint over top of the mines. Bet he got the helicopter donated. I don't want to ask. Photos of mega-projects. Engineering Feats, my foot. Open pit mines and hydro dams that'll silt-in within decades. Great Goddess, nightmare material! As if those creations were, in and of themselves, Art! Not wreaking havoc downstream or downwind, weighing down the fault lines with millions of tons of water the Earth didn't plan for.

It gives artists a bad name. Like the scientists splitting the atom, going "Wow, neato!" and then, "Gee, darn!" when the fascists and wackos obliterated human beings with the results. I don't know where he's coming from with those photos. I won't ask.

He doesn't give a damn about my work. Never asked a single question, the snot! I'm going to have a few words with Liang for lining up this precious twit with me, just because we're going to get awards at the same conference and he's our mutual gallery and, gee, wouldn't it be nice and convenient?

And me, I get sucked in because the guy's famous and talented and I'm semi-famous and underconfident! Never mind. Let it go. I'm going to drive like the devil, enjoy the Cariboò, the horses, old log barns, and get some sleep when we hit spruce country. In Dawson Creek, I'll show off the grain elevator converted to an art gallery. That'll shut him up. Not that he's talking. Let's play some Penguin Cafe Orchestra and give ourselves to the open road. Shall we, Rufus? Shake a paw on it?

THE FLOTILLA OF CANOES
Hans Richter's Slide Show

"Freddy! Bertie! Jah, good. CLICK.

"First slide of our trip. This is Frederich and Norbert beside the Twelve Foot Davis statue in Peace River, Alberta. He is a pioneer figure of wood, but this is over-exposed. A sunny day but the beginning of such a trip must be documented, yes?"

"Everybody! Raise the glasses, you too, Wolfy!" CLICK.

"Here is our picnic supper after the first day on the Peace River. We are camping right beside the river, which is quite high and very muddy. June 1st. Also, very cold, impossible to swim. But Alfred has brought champagne to celebrate."

CLICK.

"Sunset on the first night, about ten o'clock in the evening. Astounding long daylight. We were 57° latitude, approximately."

"Okay, everybody, smile big!" CLICK.

"Here we are, just about to begin our second day of paddling. Our guide is the man with the funny hat. Davy Crockett. We wanted to have canoes made the traditional way of birch bark, but he said he would only have aluminum for tourists. This is safer on rivers with rocks and trees and things. Okay, now is our second night."

"Achtung!" CLICK.

"Hah, hah, Freddie! Caught in the act. Mosquitoes bit our bums something awful. Norbert was stopped up! He couldn't go at all for the whole ten days until we got to the airport! Mother of God, can you imagine it?"

CAROLINE WOODWARD

CLICK.

"The most beautiful scenery is the wide part of the valley, but this will be flooded if the government is stupid, which it apparently is."

CLICK.

"This one is of the buildings with the waterline drawn on them, to show how far the river water would come up if the dam is constructed."

CLICK.

"Next, the old gentleman with his market garden right next to the river. Look, black land, stuff grows like crazy. Cantalopes, cucumbers, corn, tomatoes, marvelous land!"

"The map! Hold it up straight and point to where we are. Just one of you! Jah!" CLICK.

"Here is Alfred and Frederich with our waterproof map and this is the Taylor Refinery in the background. Big yellow mountains of sulphur from the gas refining plant. Stinks like hell. Our guide says it's the smell of money. Money in Canada smells like rotten eggs!"

"Hold up your glasses, smile big!" CLICK.

"Here we are in the Silver Dollar Bar and Lounge in Taylor. Incredible! All the dollars are sunk in the wall, hundreds of them. The owner, him with the moustache and the tray of beer, he said this was a big town in 1958, a hopping town, he said, when the Refinery was being built. We got very drunk that night and stayed in a motel to have hot baths. We are all growing beards for this trip, you see?"

"Wunderbar!" CLICK.

"Max and Wolfgang and Volkmar walked right under the Peace River bridge, which is between Taylor and the market gardens. See how wide it is? They are like ants!

FINDING DUE NORTH

Foolish boys, but they kept their nerve on the little walk-way underneath. When a truck or car would drive over top of them, the whole bridge would shake, shake, shake for half a kilometre!''
"Oh!'' CLICK. CLICK. CLICK. CLICK. CLICK.
"This is a deer, a whitetail, swimming across the river. See! The next four slides, I went crazy. It was my first Canadian wildlife. I just couldn't sleep, too much beer, too much early light at 3 a.m., so I took the camera down to the river, in case there was something interesting. See! There she has spotted me and she jumps into the forest in two leaps!''
"Beachboys!'' CLICK.
"Everybody got so hot, paddling the last three days, they take off their shirts, put mosquito spray all over themselves, and get sunburned instead. This is where we find out that our maps from Germany are too old. Our guide laughs his head off, like he thought we knew all along! We can't go any further because there are two dams on the Peace River. The garden people will go under if a third dam is made! So we finally understand this situation, but we have a small discussion about wages with the guide. I wanted to go along the river and follow Alexander Mac-kenzie, the famous explorer, but now it is not authentic. I want a birch canoe and a guide who does not drink so much. Alfred would like a real Indian guide, but they don't use the river anymore. They don't have canoes anymore, says this guide. However, he doesn't like Indians, so we must get second opinions.''
"Big wave, everyone!'' CLICK.
"We are now in front of the Fort St. John Tourist Office. That is a totem pole made by white people. The Indians

in this area do not make totem poles. It is not their tribal way! I studied this in Germany, and I can tell you they are hunters and gatherers. Next summer, I will come back and go to live with the Indians on my own. My English is good enough, yes? I will go to the Halfway Reserve because I saw that river, the Halfway, before we came to that dam where we had no choice but to get out of the river. I will study the Beaver and Cree languages. I will live in a tent!''
CLICK.
"This is the airport at Fort St. John. To document the end of our journey. But I must say, I am mad about exploring more! A little wild Canada for you, yes? Thank you very much, thank you!''

UP IN THE SKY
Nature Plus

On a 737 Boeing flight from Vancouver, B.C. to Fort St. John, B.C.: 84 passengers, including a nine-year-old girl and her mother coming back from the Children's Hospital (Muscular Dystrophy), a juvenile escorted by an R.C.M.P. officer for a pending trial (a massive series of b&e's, car thefts, and fraud), two nuns, a psychiatrist, eight senior citizens back from their biannual Las Vegas junket, one university drop-out, thirty-four American hunters and thirty-four men in white lab coats. Imagine that for a while.

Here's the scoop. Hunting season is about to open for big game. Elk, stone sheep, caribou, moose, deer. Moose and deer are open already, as a matter of fact. There are more telescopic rifles, Bowie knives, down vests and one hundred dollar bills than you'd see in a big-game outfitters store. We are talking arsenal here.

FINDING DUE NORTH

The fellows with the guns aren't really hunters, though. They used to be, some of them, but not anymore. They are artists. Performance artists. A jazz quintet. A guerilla theatre troupe. Poets. They dress in combat fatigues, boots, vests, and Tilley hats because they are savvy to parody. The first line of their two-act play is: "The only good thing about hunting season is that more hunters kill each other off."

The performance artists do stand-up comedy, rap poems, and choreographed dance works. They really get a stage bouncing when all six of them are clumping around in their jungle boots. "Bounty Hunter" is a sure-fire hit, dealing as it does with the fate of helicopter hunters chasing down wolves and crashing into the side of Pink Mountain. "Blood Lust" is another winner. Most of the audiences can identify with a fellow hunter and his gun going into a feeding frenzy after ten expensive days in the mountains and not a single shot fired at anything with horns. Bye, bye, camp cooks!

The musicians look like J.L. Bean catalogue models on northern safari, the slick sunglasses indoors and all that. They like to stand out a little, even in this crowd. Their drummer is live on stage, no computerized box for this band. Being jazz artists, they don't kill a lot of time on lyrics (Acka-acka-acka, gotta elk, momma elk, poppa elk, gotta getta baby elk, data-data-data), but wax eloquent with instrumentals and stagey antics. "To Kill a Whiskey Jack" really grabs the crowd by the throat. It begins with early dawn in the mountains, the rumble of thunder, and the cook announcing breakfast on the triangle, ding, ding, ding.

Here's where it gets referential. We all remember the

orchestra doing "Peter and the Wolf?" All the instruments taking on characters in the story? Anyway, these musicians perform "B.C. Biologists and the Wolves," a twist on the original tale.

The whiskey jack is a piccolo and the grizzly bear is a tuba, perfect or what? The deer is a violin and the elk is a cello. The biologists are cymbals, crashing through the bush looking for wolves to slaughter, for their own good, of course. The leaves and the wind are a harp and flute, while the piano is running water. The moose is a saxophone for the obligatory sax solo, and the loon call is performed by one of the musicians.

There are huge slides of the animals on three screens behind the band, as well as slides of dawn, sunset, scenery, pack horses, and guns for this number. It's hard to do justice to them without hearing them, but they get the crowds riled up, one way or the other, believe you me!

The theatre men present a realistic version of hunters trespassing on an Indian reserve and a farm owned by a maniacal old farmer. It's funny for a while, then it gets tragic, and then they invite the audience to be a kangaroo court to decide the fate of the trigger-happy hunters.

One actor is one-quarter Saulteaux, and he plays a Beaver Indian going out to get some food for his family the day before the hunting season is opened. Boy oh boy, this gets the crowd going too, especially when the performance is out on a reserve. The white crowds in towns just mumble to their neighbours, mumble, mumble, poaching, yeah, mumble, can't blame them, nope, mumble, here first, after all, eh?

Back to the jet, about to land in Fort St. John, circling over the plateau, over the Peace and Beatton Rivers, over the five grain elevators and the rail cars standing by for loading, back to the men in white lab coats.

This you won't believe even if you hung in there with me on the hunters in drag! Thirty-four men in lab coats with the sickly pale look of indoor workers under unhealthy fluorescent lights and photocopier fumes and worse. The truth of the matter is that these men are chemists in the labs of hair dye manufacturers down south and back east. They are on a mission.

The North and South Peace districts of B.C. possess the only true prairie in the province. It's called the Alberta Plateau, and when it isn't too dry, too wet, frosted too early, poor seeding weather, poor harvesting weather or subject to hail, it is a remarkable area for growing cereal grains and forage crops. From the air you can see a patchwork quilt of colours that are infinitely subtle and enticing to the eye. Especially if the eyes belong to hair dye industrialists whose new line is called Nature Plus. Here's the plan.

Light planes and parachutes have been rented and await the arrival of the chemists at the airport. These are solo flights. A reward is offered. Top blend. Off the jet and onto the tarmac they march, gripping their briefcases. Into light planes, where they are strapped into parachutes and issued rations and sleeping bags. One by one they take off in all directions, and at about seven thousand feet the chemists jump.

Down they waft, trailing the bright parrot colours of their chutes, drifting down like dandelion fluffs and landing like troopers onto the summerfallow, the hay fields or in between the swaths of grain. They break out easels from inside their briefcases and paint in the perfect late afternoon light. They collect samples and press them carefully onto acid-free paper. They look and look for a new blonde, a glorious brunette, a sassy redhead among the leaves and grains and plumes of brome grass.

For this is a field trip designed to refresh and renew the sagging spirits of the chemists, the men who toil in labs with vials and beakers and foul-smelling liquids. They roll in the hay, eat hard dry wheat, jump into the rivers like overweight otters; they press the colours of flowers onto paper, like Titian did centuries before for lack of paint. Fireweed, Indian paintbrush, bluebells, asters, goldenrod, they don't care if it ever comes out as hair dye. They are drunk with beauty, mad for purity.

But what the industrialists of Nature Plus hadn't counted on was the men in white coats coming back to Burnaby and Mississauga, smashing the beakers and vials, spraying graffiti like NATURE PLUS LACKS SOUL (that hurt, that really, really hurt) on the bathroom cubicles and quitting! Yes, they up and quit to become landscape painters and sculptors. Got on planes and came back north. You can spot them in fields and coulees and look-out points with their white lab coats all splotched with colour. Their cholesterol count is down, they've shed pounds, they've got wind burns and tans. They are happy at last.

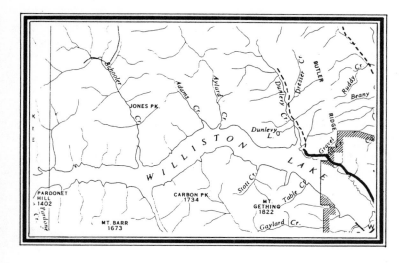

Disturbing the Peace:
A Land Quartet

ONCE '

I used to work decayed goodness
hold nodules on the roots
of legumes; alfalfa, clover, birdsfoot trefoil
charging the soil with nitrogen
planting this garden, half an acre
of potatoes flanked by sunflowers
squash, pumpkin, marrow
(Allow two yards on either side for tendrils)
giant leaves, land vines

room to move
to prosper, to break even, survive one more winter
if the first killing frost holds off

      □   □   □

I used to haul water, saw wood
feed bunting calves
bring home the *coos*
Cooo, baasss! Coooo, baasssy!
& herd them back again
back to the lease land
back to the river banks
river breaks, we call them here
sage & wild onion on the breaks
peavine in the coulees
cactus lurking on the slopes
crocus in the spring
mica glinting off the walls
of hoodoos & high earth hogsbacks
land spines slumping
breaking by the ton or a tablespoon a day
I used to leave the cattle belly high
in peavine, in the mid-summer shade
down by the saltspring
skirting the muskeg & rumours of quicksand
leave them down by the river
knee deep in brown water
brown cows with white faces on brown water
sun dappling through the Balm of Gilead leaves
on the banks of the Beatton River

      □   □   □

DISTURBING THE PEACE

I used to climb the packtrail up again
the trail worn down by padding feet
centuries of deer & moose
skinned & quartered in Killemquick Coulee
lotsa deer, kill 'em quick
that's what the Beaver man told Dad
stopping by for tea & tobacco
meat to trade, talk for a bit
before the government agent
plans kept the Beaver hunters, the Dunne'za
on some frozen chunk of land far away from this river

       □   □   □

in Killemquick Coulee the land lays exposed
silt, loam, gravel, gumbo, humus
ancient jungle compressed far below
lakes of sour gas & superheated water
the plateau above carved by rivers
covered in trees or prairies turned to fields
or foothills of the northern Rockies
"First Animals Sleeping"
say the Dunne'za
pointing to the blue hills folding away & up into blue clouds
away from the river where dinosaurs danced
did the three-toed Pre-Cambrian shuffle
once

       □   □   □

TWO DECADES LATER

They say it's the big lake
the Dam Lake
four hundred miles long

CAROLINE WOODWARD

drowning tree trunks & fence posts
standing still & straight
beside fields & pastures
drowning fossil footprints of dinosaur
deer trails, wagon tracks, roads
silting over bones all bunched
up in box canyons
old look-out points look out to see
only green water
swirling up deadhead logs
looming black & malevolent

there's a milltown at one end of the lake
instant asphalt crescents
shopping mall, curling rink
in the middle of coniferous bush

Funny, this new weather though
winters all icefog, strange stuff
summers colder, shorter somehow
they say it's the big lake
doomed to seventy years maybe
before the silt blocks in the turbines solid
& the Dam grinds to a halt
& then the silt that smothered the screaming bones
of deer & bear & lynx & moose & nesting birds
& resting spirits will settle
into a proper grave
under the strangled flow
of the River

☐   ☐   ☐

TRIO FOR VOICES

We're the hinterland
we warm you there down south
winter people go cabin crazy
in our double-wides & company houses
but isolation pays well
overtime stories fly high as the bottles
in the bars & cabarets
we only got a couple dentists
lots of cops
one flying shrink
3.5 days a month
book now
avoid disappointment
check out the roughnecks off the rigs
in the cabarets
danger pay in their pockets
semen leaking from their eyes
exotic dancers up from Edmonton
for a gig in the John
Foreskin John.

□   □   □

Mennonite women still walk
in mud-spattered housedresses
behind their men, tow-headed children in between
old-timers congregate for coffee
in the Co-op, two bits a cup
Indians from the Doig, the Blueberry or Halfway
stalk the aisles of the I.G.A.
town food

CAROLINE WOODWARD

wieners & beans
eaten cold in empty lots
ducked down in high dead grass

◻   ◻   ◻

Oil execs in cowboy boots
date razzle dazzle real estate ladies
farm women save coupons
eye ready-made racks
think maybe this fall
a wedding
& move on to yard goods
move on like everyone's son in a 4X4
& everybody, everyday
gets wide sky country radio
with Genial Gene yer host
& message time for all you truckers
& travellers up the Alcan
"Millie, bring down the horses to mile 95
we'll meet you round noon tomorrow
with the groceries
that's from Billy & Jim"
radio waves bouncing clear as a bell
to Pink Mountain, rainshadow of the Rockies
good chinook country
but an ill wind whistles these days
down empty rows of condos
& emptier dead soldiers
twenty-sixers of rye in the ditches
& Old Man Lewis, what a joker
got this photo at brother Alf's stag
lampshade hanging off his head

DISTURBING THE PEACE

pissed to the gills
his widow's got instructions
day after the funeral, buy a big ad
Alaska Highway News eh
LORDY, LORDY
LOOK WHO'S DEAD
& signs say OUT OF WORK,
MOVING, MUST SELL,
IN RECEIVERSHIP, ALL ASSETS FROZEN
(Hide the silver, Honey, the sheriff's at the door!)
& highrollers sashay down the white lines
do the boom & bust balancing act
split the profits
cut the take
take your cut
head south

□ □ □

THREE-QUARTER TIME

Who says
dam the river, damn it, dam it again?
Who says
If it can't grow & it doesn't move, mine it?
Who says
call the banks on their interests?
Who says
kneel down
hold topsoil
decayed goodness
in both hands
Who says
keep this earth
in good hands?

Other titles in the Polestar First Fiction Series:

Mobile Homes
Noel Hudson
"a brilliant first collection of comic offbeat stories"

Ten Dollars and a Dream
Hazel Jameson
"a novel of courage and dignity set in Alberta during the 1930s"

The Tasmanian Tiger
Jane Barker Wright
"Motherhood. Mystery. Murder. A powerful first novel."

Fall 1990
Rapid Transits and Other Stories
Holley Rubinsky
"award-winning stories by the first Journey prize winner"

Other fine contemporary fiction and poetry from Polestar Press:

Song to the Rising Sun
Paulette Jiles

The Jesse James Poems
Paulette Jiles

Sitting in the Club Car Drinking Rum & Karma Kola
Paulette Jiles

Bloodsong and Other Stories of South Africa
Ernst Havemann

A Labour of Love
edited by Mona Fertig

The Rocket, the Flower, the Hammer and Me
edited by Doug Beardsley

Vancouver Poetry
edited by Allan Safarik

Vancouver Fiction
edited by David Watmough

Being On the Moon
Annharte

An X-Ray of Longing
Glen Downie

North Book
Jim Green

Castle Mountain
Luanne Armstrong